Bernice Bobs Her Hair

*Jazz-Age Transformations, Ambition
& Social Competition in a Dazzling
American Summer*

A Modern Translation
Adapted for the Contemporary Reader

F. Scott Fitzgerald

Translated by Tim Zengerink

Table of Contents

Preface
Message to the Reader

Rebuilding the Greatest Library in Human History

Thousands of years ago, the Library of Alexandria was the heart of global knowledge — a sanctuary where the wisdom of every known civilization was gathered and shared freely.

And then, it was lost.

Now, we're rebuilding it — and you are invited to join us.

At the Library of Alexandria, we've set out to make every book available to every person on Earth — not just in print, but in every language, every format, and for every reader.

Here's how we do it:

- **Deluxe Print Editions at True Printing Cost** - Order any book as a high-quality paperback, elegant hardcover, or stunning boxset — and only pay what it costs to print. No markups. No middlemen.
- **Unlimited Access to the Greatest Works** - Enjoy thousands of timeless classics — from Plato to Shakespeare to Tolstoy — in beautiful, modern eBook and audiobook editions. Read and listen without limits — for every reader, everywhere.
- **Modern Translations for Every Language & Dialect** - We're reimagining the classics in clear, accessible language — and translating them into every dialect imaginable. Everyone deserves to understand humanity's greatest ideas.

When you visit **LibraryofAlexandria.com**, you're not just accessing books — you're joining a global movement to restore, preserve, and share the wisdom of civilization.

Join us today at LibraryofAlexandria.com

Together, we'll ensure the light of human wisdom never fades again.

With gratitude,

The Modern Library of Alexandria Team

Visit:
www.libraryofalexandria.com
Or scan the code below:

Introduction

The Jazz Age and Fitzgerald's Sharp Eye on Society

Few writers have captured the sparkle, ambition, and social undercurrents of the Jazz Age as brilliantly as F. Scott Fitzgerald. His short story Bernice Bobs Her Hair, first published in The Saturday Evening Post on May 1, 1920, remains one of the defining works of this era. It's a story that blends wit, social critique, and a razor-sharp look at the dynamics of popularity, femininity, and personal transformation in early 20th-century America. On the surface, the tale revolves around a seemingly trivial event—a young woman cutting her hair—but beneath this simple premise lies a rich exploration of identity, gender roles, and the tension between authenticity and social expectation.

Set against the backdrop of a glittering American summer, Bernice Bobs Her Hair introduces readers to Bernice, a shy and somewhat awkward young woman visiting her sophisticated and socially savvy cousin, Marjorie Harvey. Bernice's world is one where popularity and charm are currency, and young women are expected to navigate the treacherous waters of social gatherings, dances, and flirtations with effortless grace. Unfortunately for Bernice, her lack of confidence and outdated conversational style make her an outsider in this competitive world. Marjorie, ever conscious of her own social standing, decides to take Bernice under her wing, giving her a crash course in the art of attracting attention and admiration.

Under Marjorie's guidance, Bernice undergoes a remarkable transformation. She learns how to engage in witty banter, flirt strategically, and exude the confidence expected of a young woman of her time. Her newfound charm quickly wins her popularity among the local young men, including Warren, one of Marjorie's admirers. This shift in social dynamics sets the stage for a subtle yet intense rivalry between the two cousins. What began as an act of charity on Marjorie's part soon turns into jealousy and competition, as Bernice's star begins to rise at Marjorie's expense.

The story's pivotal moment comes when Bernice, in an attempt to cement her newfound popularity, agrees to carry out a bold and scandalous act for the time: bobbing her hair. In the 1920s, bobbed hair symbolized rebellion and modernity, a departure from the long, traditional hairstyles that had dominated Victorian and Edwardian ideals of femininity. To bob one's hair was to embrace the spirit of the "New Woman"—independent, daring, and willing to defy convention. For Bernice, this decision represents both a culmination of her transformation and a personal leap into self-determination. Yet the reaction to her haircut is not what she expects. Instead of admiration, she faces ridicule and rejection, exposing the superficial and fickle nature of the social world she has fought so hard to conquer.

The brilliance of Bernice Bobs Her Hair lies not only in its depiction of social rivalry but also in its underlying critique of the shallow values that govern the pursuit of popularity. Fitzgerald's narrative, laced with both humor and irony, exposes the performative nature of social interactions—how charm and confidence are often constructed rather than innate, and how quickly admiration can turn to scorn when the rules of the game are not carefully followed. Bernice's journey is at once triumphant and tragic. While she successfully reinvents herself, she also learns the harsh reality that social approval is fleeting and conditional.

Yet Bernice is far from a passive victim of this world. In the story's final, unforgettable act, she takes her revenge on Marjorie in a way that is both shocking and empowering. This moment, both humorous and cathartic, cements Bernice as one of Fitzgerald's most memorable heroines— a character who, despite her initial insecurities, ultimately asserts her own agency in a world that seeks to define and confine her.

Themes of Identity, Gender, and Social Ambition

Bernice Bobs Her Hair is much more than a story about a haircut; it is a commentary on the construction of identity and the pressures placed on young women in the early 20th century. The Jazz Age, with its emphasis on modernity, freedom, and self-expression, offered new opportunities for women to challenge traditional roles. Yet these opportunities often came with their own set of expectations. Women were encouraged to be bold and stylish, but only within the limits set by societal norms. Fitzgerald captures this paradox perfectly through the character of Marjorie, who embodies the ideal of the socially adept young woman—confident, fashionable, and quick-witted—but who is also deeply calculating and manipulative.

Bernice's transformation highlights the tension between authenticity and performance. At the start of the story, Bernice is sincere but socially awkward, failing to conform to the "rules" of popularity. With Marjorie's help, she learns to adopt the behaviors and attitudes that society rewards. But in doing so, she also loses a part of her true self, becoming a character in a carefully orchestrated performance. Her decision to bob her hair—a moment of genuine boldness—marks a turning point where she attempts to assert her individuality, but the negative reaction she receives underscores how precarious and unforgiving social approval can be.

The story also explores themes of rivalry and female relationships. Marjorie's mentorship of Bernice is not entirely selfless; it is motivated by a desire to maintain control over her social sphere. When Bernice's success begins to overshadow her own, Marjorie turns against her cousin, exposing the competitive undercurrents that often lie beneath seemingly friendly interactions. This dynamic reflects broader societal pressures that pit women against each other in the pursuit of male attention and validation, a theme that remains relevant even today.

Another important theme is the role of appearance and fashion as markers of identity. In the 1920s, bobbed hair was more than a mere style choice—it was a symbol of liberation and rebellion. Women who cut their hair short were often seen as modern, daring, and even scandalous. By choosing to bob her hair, Bernice is not only making a personal statement but also engaging with a broader cultural shift. Her transformation mirrors the changing attitudes of the time, as women began to challenge traditional ideals of beauty and femininity.

Fitzgerald's writing is particularly effective in capturing the nuances of social interaction. His sharp observations and witty dialogue bring to life the world of summer dances, porch conversations, and competitive charm. Every gesture, every word is a calculated move in the social game, and

Fitzgerald's keen eye for detail makes this world feel both glamorous and absurd. Through Bernice's eyes, readers see the allure of popularity but also its emptiness—the way it demands constant performance and offers little in the way of genuine connection or fulfillment.

Fitzgerald's Social Commentary and Lasting Legacy

F. Scott Fitzgerald is often remembered as the chronicler of the Jazz Age, a writer who captured both its dazzling surface and its underlying tensions. Bernice Bobs Her Hair is a perfect example of his ability to weave social commentary into a compelling narrative. While the story is entertaining and even comedic, it also raises serious questions about the nature of identity, the costs of conformity, and the fleeting nature of social success.

In many ways, Bernice's story is a microcosm of the themes that would define Fitzgerald's later works, including The Great Gatsby. Both stories explore the pursuit of acceptance and recognition in a world driven by appearances and status. Both also highlight the gap between the idealized version of oneself that one presents to the world and the deeper, more complicated self that lies beneath. For Bernice, as for many of Fitzgerald's characters, the quest for social validation is both intoxicating and destructive.

The story's conclusion is particularly striking in its refusal to offer a neat resolution. While Bernice's act of revenge on Marjorie provides a moment of satisfaction, it does not erase the complexities of her journey. She emerges from the story not as a triumphant heroine but as a young woman who has glimpsed both the power and the emptiness of social approval. In this sense, Bernice Bobs Her Hair is both a cautionary tale and a story of self-discovery.

The historical context of the story adds another layer of richness. The 1920s were a time of dramatic social change in America. Women were gaining greater independence, both politically (with the ratification of the 19th Amendment in 1920) and socially, as they embraced new fashions, new freedoms, and new roles. The flapper, with her short skirts, bobbed hair, and bold attitude, became a symbol of this new era. By placing Bernice's transformation within this cultural moment, Fitzgerald not only tells a personal story but also comments on a broader shift in American values and identity.

Today, Bernice Bobs Her Hair remains as relevant as ever. While the specifics of social life have changed, the pressures to conform, to perform, and to seek validation from others are still very much present. In a world of social media, where image and popularity are often measured by likes and followers, Bernice's struggle to define herself in the face of external judgment feels strikingly modern. Fitzgerald's story reminds us that the quest for acceptance, while deeply human, can also be fraught with challenges and compromises.

Bernice Bobs Her Hair

Chapter 1

After dark on Saturday night, you could stand on the first tee of the golf course and see the country club windows glowing like a yellow expanse above a very black and rolling ocean. The waves of this ocean, so to speak, were the heads of many curious caddies, a few of the more clever chauffeurs, the golf professional's deaf sister—and there were usually several scattered, hesitant waves who could have gone inside if they had wanted to. This was the gallery.

The balcony was located indoors. It was made up of a circle of wicker chairs arranged along the wall of the room that served as both a clubroom and ballroom. During these Saturday evening dances, it was mostly occupied by women—a loud gathering of middle-aged ladies with keen eyes and cold hearts, peering through their opera glasses while displaying their ample figures. The balcony's primary purpose was to judge and criticize; it might occasionally show reluctant admiration, but never genuine approval, since it's common knowledge among women over thirty-five that when young people dance during the summer, they have the most improper intentions imaginable, and without the watchful glare of disapproving eyes, wandering couples would perform strange, wild dance sequences in dark corners, while the more sought-after and therefore more threatening young women might find themselves being kissed in the parked luxury cars belonging to unsuspecting wealthy older ladies.

But ultimately, this critical circle isn't positioned close enough to the stage to observe the actors' expressions and notice the more subtle interactions. It can only scowl and lean forward, pose questions and draw reasonable conclusions from its established assumptions, like the belief that every young man with substantial wealth lives like a hunted bird. It never truly grasps the drama of the changing, somewhat harsh world of teenage years. No; let the theater boxes, orchestra section, leading performers, and supporting cast be represented by the mixture of faces and voices that move to the melancholy African beat of Dyer's dance band.

From sixteen-year-old Otis Ormonde, who still has two more years left at Hill School, to G. Reece Stoddard, whose Harvard law diploma hangs prominently above the dresser in his bedroom at home; from young Madeleine Hogue, whose hair still feels awkward and unfamiliar piled up on her head, to Bessie MacRae, who has been the center of attention at parties for far too long—more than a decade now—this diverse group not only occupies the spotlight but consists of the only individuals who can see the stage clearly without anything blocking their view.

With a dramatic flourish and sudden crash, the music comes to an abrupt halt. The dancing couples flash fake, practiced smiles at each other, playfully echoing "la-de-da-da dum-dum," while the chatter of young women's voices rises above the eruption of applause.

A few disappointed young men caught in the middle of the dance floor as they were about to cut in drifted back to the walls without enthusiasm, because this wasn't like the wild Christmas dances—these summer dances were considered just pleasantly warm and exciting, where even the younger married couples got up and performed old-fashioned waltzes and intimidating fox trots to the patient amusement of their younger brothers and sisters.

Warren McIntyre, who had casually attended Yale and found himself among the unlucky men without dates, reached into his tuxedo pocket for a cigarette and wandered out onto the broad, dimly lit veranda, where couples sat scattered at tables, filling the lantern-lit night with soft conversations and muffled laughter. He acknowledged various people as he walked by the less engrossed couples, and as he passed each pair, some half-remembered piece of gossip surfaced in his thoughts, since it wasn't a large city and everyone knew everyone else's history. There, for instance, sat Jim Strain and Ethel Demorest, who had been secretly engaged for three years. Everyone understood that the moment Jim could keep a job for longer than two months, she would marry him. Still, how bored they both appeared, and how tiredly Ethel sometimes looked at Jim, as though she questioned why she had wrapped her feelings around such an unsteady foundation.

Warren was nineteen and felt somewhat sorry for his friends who hadn't headed east for college. However, like most young men, he boasted endlessly about the girls from his hometown whenever he was away. There was Genevieve Ormonde, who consistently attended dances, house parties, and football games at Princeton, Yale, Williams, and Cornell; there was dark-eyed Roberta Dillon, who was just as well-known among her peers as Hiram Johnson or Ty Cobb; and naturally, there was Marjorie Harvey, who not only possessed an enchanting face and a brilliant, captivating way with words but had already earned well-deserved fame for performing five consecutive cartwheels during the recent informal dance at New Haven.

Warren, who had grown up across the street from Marjorie, had been head over heels for her for years. Sometimes she seemed to return his feelings with mild appreciation, but she had put him through her foolproof test and told him seriously that she didn't love him. Her test was simple: when she was away from him, she forgot about him and dated other guys. Warren found this disheartening, especially since Marjorie had been taking short trips all summer, and for the first few days after each time she came home, he noticed large piles of mail on the Harveys' front hall table addressed to her in different men's handwriting. To make things even worse, throughout the entire month of August she had been hosting her cousin Bernice from Eau Claire, and it seemed impossible to get her alone. It was always necessary to search around and find someone to keep Bernice company. As August came to an end, this was becoming increasingly difficult.

Although Warren adored Marjorie, he had to acknowledge that Cousin Bernice was rather dull. She was attractive, with dark hair and a vibrant complexion, but she wasn't enjoyable at parties. Every Saturday night he endured a long, tedious obligatory dance with her to make Marjorie happy, but he had never felt anything other than boredom when he was with her.

"Warren"—a gentle voice beside him interrupted his thoughts, and he turned to find Marjorie, glowing and vibrant as always. She placed her hand on his shoulder, and warmth spread through him almost without him noticing.

"Warren," she whispered, "do something for me— dance with Bernice. She's been stuck with little Otis Ormonde for almost an hour."

Warren's glow faded.

"Why—sure," he replied without much enthusiasm.

"You don't mind, do you? I'll make sure you don't get stuck."

"'S all right."

Marjorie smiled—that smile that was thanks enough.

"You're an angel, and I owe you big time."

With a sigh, the angel looked around the veranda, but Bernice and Otis were nowhere to be seen. He wandered back inside, and there in front of the women's dressing room he discovered Otis at the center of a group of young men who were doubled over with laughter. Otis was waving around a piece of wood he had grabbed, talking animatedly.

"She went inside to fix her hair," he said excitedly. "I'm waiting so I can dance with her for another hour."

Their laughter started up again.

"Why don't some of you cut in?" Otis called out with irritation. "She enjoys more variety."

"Why, Otis," a friend suggested, "you've just barely gotten used to her."

"Why the two-by-four, Otis?" Warren asked with a smile.

"The two-by-four? Oh, this? This is a club. When she comes out I'll hit her on the head and knock her in again."

Warren collapsed onto a couch and burst into delighted laughter.

"Don't worry about it, Otis," he said at last. "I'm letting you off the hook this time."

Otis pretended to suddenly faint and gave the stick to Warren.

"If you need it, old man," he said in a rough voice.

No matter how beautiful or intelligent a girl might be, having a reputation for not being frequently asked to dance by different partners puts her in an awkward position at a dance. Perhaps boys enjoy her company more than that of the popular girls they dance with countless times during an evening, but young people in this jazz-influenced generation are naturally restless by nature, and the thought of dancing more than one complete dance with the same girl is unpleasant, even repulsive. When it comes to multiple dances and the breaks between them, she can be certain that once a young man gets away, he will never step on her unpredictable feet again.

Warren danced the entire next dance with Bernice, and when it ended, he gratefully took advantage of the break to escort her to a table on the porch. They sat in silence for a moment while she fidgeted awkwardly with her fan.

"It's hotter here than in Eau Claire," she said.

Warren held back a sigh and nodded. For all he knew or cared, that might well be true. He found himself wondering whether she was bad at conversation because no one paid attention to her, or if no one paid attention to her because she was bad at conversation.

"Are you planning to stay here much longer?" he asked, then felt his face flush red. She might figure out why he was asking.

"Another week," she replied, fixing him with a stare as though ready to pounce on whatever words came out of his mouth next.

Warren shifted restlessly. Then, struck by a sudden generous impulse, he decided to test part of his approach on her. He turned and looked into her eyes.

"You have an incredibly kissable mouth," he said softly.

This was something he would sometimes say to girls at college dances when they were talking in this same kind of dim lighting. Bernice visibly startled. Her face turned an awkward shade of red and she fumbled clumsily with her fan. No one had ever said anything like that to her before.

13

"Fresh!"—the word escaped her lips before she could stop herself, and she quickly bit down on her lower lip. Realizing it was too late to take it back, she chose to find the situation amusing instead and gave him a flustered smile.

Warren felt irritated. While he wasn't used to having that comment taken seriously, it typically sparked laughter or some playful, sentimental teasing. He despised being called fresh, unless it was meant as a joke. His generous impulse faded away and he changed the subject.

"Jim Strain and Ethel Demorest are sitting out as usual," he remarked.

This was more suited to Bernice's comfort zone, but a slight sense of regret mixed with her relief as the conversation shifted to a different topic. Men didn't speak to her about lips worth kissing, but she was aware that they spoke in similar ways to other girls.

"Oh, yes," she said, and laughed. "I hear they've been wandering around for years without any money at all. Isn't it ridiculous?"

Warren's disgust grew stronger. Jim Strain was a close friend of his brother, and besides, he thought it was poor manners to mock people for lacking money. However, Bernice hadn't meant to be mocking at all. She was simply anxious.

Chapter 2

When Marjorie and Bernice arrived home at twelve-thirty in the morning, they said goodnight at the top of the staircase. Although they were cousins, they weren't close friends. Actually, Marjorie didn't have any close female friends—she thought girls were foolish. Bernice, on the other hand, had hoped throughout this visit that her parents had arranged to share those intimate conversations filled with laughter and tears that she believed were essential to all relationships between women. However, she discovered that Marjorie was quite distant in this regard; she somehow felt the same challenge in speaking with her that she experienced when talking to men. Marjorie never laughed in that giggly way, was never scared, rarely felt awkward, and truthfully possessed very few of the traits that Bernice viewed as properly and wonderfully feminine.

As Bernice went through her nightly routine with her toothbrush and toothpaste, she found herself wondering for the hundredth time why she never received any attention when she was away from home. It never crossed her mind that her family's status as the wealthiest in Eau Claire might be a factor in her hometown social success, or that her mother's lavish entertaining, the intimate dinner parties she threw for her daughter before every dance, and the car she had bought for her to drive around town all played a role. Like most young women of her generation, she had grown up reading the wholesome stories of Annie Fellows Johnston and novels where the heroine was adored for certain mysterious feminine qualities that were always referenced but never actually shown.

Bernice felt a nagging sense that she wasn't currently enjoying any real popularity. She had no idea that without Marjorie's behind-the-scenes efforts, she would have spent the whole evening dancing with just one partner; however, she was aware that even back in Eau Claire, other girls who had less social standing and weren't as attractive received far more attention from men. She blamed this on something quietly dishonest about those girls. This had never bothered her before, and if it ever had, her mother would have reassured her that those other girls were lowering their standards and that men truly respected girls like Bernice.

She switched off the bathroom light and, acting on a whim, decided to visit her aunt Josephine for a brief conversation, noticing that her light remained on. Her soft slippers carried her silently along the carpeted hallway, but when she heard voices from within, she paused near the partially open door. She then heard her own name mentioned, and without deliberately intending to listen in, she remained there—and the flow of conversation taking place inside cut through her awareness as sharply as if it had been threaded through with a needle.

"She's completely hopeless!" Marjorie's voice rang out. "Oh, I know exactly what you're about to say! So many people have told you how beautiful and charming she is, and what a wonderful cook she is! So what? She has terrible luck with relationships. Men just don't like her."

"What's a little cheap popularity?"

Mrs. Harvey sounded irritated.

"It means everything when you're eighteen," Marjorie said with emphasis. "I've done everything I could. I've been courteous and I've gotten men to dance with her, but they simply won't tolerate being bored. When I consider that beautiful coloring being wasted on such a fool, and imagine what Martha Carey could accomplish with it—oh!"

"There's no courtesy these days."

Mrs. Harvey's tone suggested that today's circumstances were overwhelming for her. During her youth, all young women from respectable families enjoyed wonderful experiences.

"Well," said Marjorie, "no girl can keep propping up a struggling visitor forever, because nowadays it's every woman for herself. I've even tried dropping hints about clothing and other things, and she's gotten angry—shot me the strangest looks. She's perceptive enough to realize she's not making much of an impression, but I'm sure she comforts herself by believing that she's very moral and that I'm too carefree and shallow and will meet a terrible fate. All unpopular girls think like that. Sour grapes! Sarah Hopkins calls Genevieve and Roberta and me gardenia girls! I bet she'd trade ten years of her life and her European education to be a gardenia girl and have three or four men in love with her and get cut in on every few steps at dances."

"It seems to me," Mrs. Harvey interrupted with a somewhat tired tone, "that you should be able to help Bernice in some way. I realize she's not particularly lively."

Marjorie groaned.

"Lively! Oh please! I've never heard her say anything to a guy except that it's hot or the dance floor's packed or that she's going to college in New York next year. Sometimes she asks them what kind of car they drive and tells them what kind she has. How exciting!"

There was a brief silence, and then Mrs. Harvey resumed her familiar complaint:

"All I know is that other girls who aren't nearly as sweet and attractive manage to find partners. Take Martha Carey, for example—she's heavy and loud, and her mother is clearly from a lower social class. Roberta Dillon has become so thin this year that she looks like she belongs in Arizona for her health. She's literally dancing herself to death."

"But, Mom," Marjorie protested impatiently, "Martha is cheerful and incredibly funny and a really cool girl, and Roberta's an amazing dancer. She's been popular for years!"

Mrs. Harvey yawned.

"I think it's that wild Indian heritage in Bernice," Marjorie went on. "Maybe she's reverting back to her

17

ancestral nature. Native American women all just sat around and never spoke."

"Go to bed, you silly child," Mrs. Harvey laughed. "I wouldn't have told you that story if I had known you were going to remember it. And I think most of your ideas are completely ridiculous," she said drowsily.

There was another silence, while Marjorie thought about whether convincing her mother was worth the effort. People over forty can rarely be permanently convinced of anything. At eighteen our beliefs are hills from which we observe; at forty-five they are caves in which we take shelter.

Having made this decision, Marjorie said good night. When she stepped out into the hallway, it was completely empty.

Chapter 3

While Marjorie was having a late breakfast the next day, Bernice entered the room with a somewhat stiff good morning greeting, sat down across from her, and stared directly at her while slightly wetting her lips.

"What are you thinking about?" Marjorie asked, looking somewhat confused.

Bernice hesitated before she threw her hand grenade.

"I heard what you said about me to your mother last night."

Marjorie was surprised, but she only showed a slightly deeper flush in her cheeks and her voice remained completely steady when she spoke.

"Where were you?"

"In the hall. I didn't intend to eavesdrop—not initially."

After giving him an involuntary look of contempt, Marjorie looked down and became very focused on balancing a stray corn flake on her finger.

"I suppose I should just go back to Eau Claire—if I'm being such a bother." Bernice's lower lip shook uncontrollably as she went on in a shaky voice: "I've done my best to be pleasant, and—and I've been ignored first and then insulted. No visitor has ever been treated so poorly."

Marjorie remained quiet.

"But I can see I'm getting in your way. I'm holding you back. Your friends don't like me." She stopped for a moment, then recalled another complaint she had. "Naturally I was angry last week when you tried to suggest that the dress didn't look good on me. Don't you think I know how to dress myself?"

"No," he whispered barely audibly.

"What?"

"I didn't hint anything," Marjorie said bluntly. "What I said, if I recall correctly, was that it's better to wear an attractive dress three times in a row than to switch between it and two hideous ones."

"Do you think that was a very nice thing to say?"

"I wasn't trying to be nice." Then after a pause: "When do you want to go?"

Bernice drew in her breath sharply.

"Oh!" It was a small, stifled cry.

Marjorie looked up in surprise.

"Didn't you say you were going?"

"Yes, but——"

"Oh, you were only bluffing!"

They looked at each other across the breakfast table for a moment. Hazy waves drifted in front of Bernice's vision, while Marjorie's face showed that somewhat stern expression she wore when slightly drunk college students were trying to romance her.

"So you were bluffing," she said again, as though it was exactly what she had anticipated.

Bernice confessed by breaking down in tears. Marjorie's eyes revealed her boredom.

"You're my cousin," Bernice sobbed. "I'm visiting you. I was supposed to stay for a month, and if I go home my mother will find out and she'll wonder——"

Marjorie waited until the flood of fragmented words dissolved into quiet sobs.

"I'll give you my monthly allowance," she said coldly, "and you can spend this final week wherever you'd like. There's a really nice hotel——"

Bernice's crying grew higher and more piercing, like the sound of a flute, and suddenly she jumped up and ran from the room.

An hour later, while Marjorie sat in the library completely focused on writing one of those vague and wonderfully evasive letters that only a young woman can compose, Bernice came back, her eyes clearly red from crying, and deliberately trying to appear calm. She didn't look at Marjorie at all but grabbed a book randomly from the shelf and sat down as though she planned to read it. Marjorie appeared completely engrossed in her letter and kept writing. When the clock struck noon, Bernice shut her book with a sharp snap.

"I suppose I'd better get my railroad ticket."

This wasn't how she had planned to start the speech she had practiced upstairs, but since Marjorie wasn't giving her the expected responses—wasn't encouraging her to be sensible; it's a mistake—this was the best opening she could come up with.

"Just wait until I finish this letter," said Marjorie without looking around. "I want to get it sent out in the next mail."

After another minute, during which her pen scratched busily across the paper, she turned around and relaxed with an attitude that said "at your service." Once again Bernice had to speak.

"Do you want me to go home?"

"Well," said Marjorie, thinking it over, "I guess if you're not enjoying yourself you should probably leave. There's no point in being miserable."

"Don't you think common kindness——"

"Oh, please don't quote 'Little Women'!" Marjorie exclaimed with frustration. "That's completely outdated."

"You think so?"

"Good heavens, yes! What modern girl could live like those mindless women?"

"They served as role models for our mothers."

Marjorie laughed.

"Yes, they were—not! Besides, our mothers were all very well in their way, but they know very little about their daughters' problems."

Bernice straightened herself up.

"Please don't talk about my mother."

Marjorie laughed.

"I don't think I mentioned her."

Bernice felt that she was being led away from her subject.

"Do you think you've treated me very well?"

"I've done my best. You're rather difficult material to work with."

Bernice's eyelids turned red.

"I think you're cold and self-centered, and you don't have a single feminine quality about you."

"Oh, my God!" Marjorie cried out in frustration. "You're completely clueless! Girls like you are the reason for all these boring, lifeless marriages and all those awful weaknesses that people mistake for feminine virtues. What a crushing disappointment it must be when a man with vision marries the gorgeous fashion plate he's been idealizing, only to discover she's nothing but a pathetic, complaining, spineless collection of fake behaviors!"

Bernice's mouth had fallen halfway open.

"The womanly woman!" Marjorie went on. "She spends her entire youth complaining and criticizing girls like me who actually know how to enjoy ourselves."

Bernice's mouth dropped open even wider as Marjorie's voice grew louder.

"There's some excuse for an unattractive girl complaining. If I had been hopelessly ugly, I would never have forgiven my parents for bringing me into this world. But you're beginning life without any disadvantage—" Marjorie's small fist clenched, "If you expect me to cry with you, you'll be disappointed. Leave or stay, whatever you prefer." And gathering up her letters, she left the room.

Bernice said she had a headache and didn't show up for lunch. They were supposed to go to a matinée that afternoon, but since the headache continued, Marjorie had to explain the situation to a boy who didn't seem too disappointed. When she came back late in the afternoon, she discovered Bernice waiting for her in her bedroom with an oddly determined expression on her face.

"I've decided," Bernice began without any introduction, "that you might be right about things—though maybe not.

22

But if you tell me why your friends don't seem interested in me, I'll see if I can do what you're asking me to do."

Marjorie stood at the mirror, letting her hair fall loose.

"Do you mean it?"

"Yes."

"Without any hesitation? Will you do exactly what I tell you?"

"Well, I——"

"Well nothing! Will you do exactly as I say?"

"If they're sensible things."

"They're not! You have no appreciation for practical matters."

"Are you going to make—to recommend——"

"Yes, everything. If I tell you to take boxing lessons, you'll have to do it. Write home and tell your mother you're going to stay another two weeks."

"If you'll tell me——"

"Alright—let me give you a few examples. First, you don't have a natural, relaxed way about you. Why is that? It's because you're constantly worried about how you look. When a woman feels completely confident in her grooming and outfit, she can stop thinking about those things. That's what creates charm. The more aspects of yourself you can stop worrying about, the more charming you become."

"Don't I look all right?"

"No; for example, you never take care of your eyebrows. They're black and shiny, but because you leave them messy, they look bad. They would be beautiful if you spent just one-tenth of the time caring for them that you spend doing nothing. You're going to brush them so they'll grow straight."

Bernice raised her eyebrows questioningly.

"Are you telling me that men actually pay attention to eyebrows?"

"Yes—subconsciously. And when you go home you should get your teeth straightened a bit. It's barely noticeable, but still——"

"But I thought," Bernice interrupted in confusion, "that you looked down on those delicate, feminine little things."

"I can't stand delicate, overly refined thinking," Marjorie replied. "But a woman needs to be elegant in her appearance. If she looks absolutely stunning, she can discuss Russia, ping-pong, or the League of Nations and nobody will question it."

"What else?"

"Oh, I'm just getting started! There's your dancing."

"Don't I dance all right?"

"No, you don't—you lean on a man; yes, you do—just a little bit. I saw it when we were dancing together yesterday. And you dance standing completely upright instead of leaning forward slightly. Some older woman watching from the sidelines probably once told you that you looked so elegant that way. But unless you're dancing with a very petite girl, it's much more difficult for the man, and he's the one who matters."

"Go on." Bernice's mind was spinning.

"Listen, you need to learn how to be kind to guys who aren't the most confident. You act like you've been offended whenever you're stuck with anyone except the most popular boys. Look, Bernice, I get cut in on every few minutes—and who's doing most of the cutting? Those same awkward guys. No girl can afford to ignore them. They make up the majority of any group. Young men who are too shy to speak are the perfect practice for conversation. Clumsy dancers are the best practice for dancing. If you can follow their lead and still look elegant, you could follow a baby tank across a barbed-wire skyscraper."

Bernice let out a deep sigh, but Marjorie wasn't finished yet.

"If you attend a dance and genuinely entertain, let's say, three wallflowers who dance with you; if you engage them in such good conversation that they forget they're settling for you as a partner, you've accomplished something meaningful. They'll return the next time, and slowly so many of these overlooked girls will want to dance with you that the popular guys will realize there's no risk of being left with an undesirable partner—then they'll ask you to dance."

"Yes," Bernice agreed quietly. "I think I'm starting to understand."

"And finally," Marjorie concluded, "poise and charm will simply come naturally. You'll wake up one morning knowing you've achieved it, and men will recognize it too."

Bernice stood up.

"You've been incredibly kind to me—but no one has ever spoken to me this way before, and I feel somewhat surprised."

Marjorie didn't respond but stared thoughtfully at her reflection in the mirror.

"You're a peach to help me," Bernice continued.

Still Marjorie didn't respond, and Bernice felt she had appeared overly thankful.

"I know you don't like emotional displays," she said hesitantly.

Marjorie turned to her quickly.

"Oh, I wasn't thinking about that. I was wondering if we should cut your hair short."

Bernice fell back onto the bed.

Chapter 4

On the following Wednesday evening, there was a dinner-dance at the country club. When the guests walked in, Bernice found her place card with a slight feeling of annoyance. Although G. Reece Stoddard, a highly desirable and distinguished young bachelor, sat to her right, the all-important left seat was occupied only by Charley Paulson. Charley was short, plain, and lacked social skills, and with her newfound awareness, Bernice realized that his only qualification to be her dinner partner was that he had never been stuck sitting with her before. However, this feeling of annoyance disappeared as the soup course ended, and Marjorie's specific instructions came back to her. Swallowing her pride, she turned to Charley Paulson and dove in.

"Do you think I should cut my hair short, Mr. Charley Paulson?"

Charley looked up in surprise.

"Why?"

"Because I'm thinking about it. It's such a reliable and simple way to get people's attention."

Charley smiled warmly. He had no way of knowing this conversation had been practiced beforehand. He responded by saying he didn't understand much about short hair. However, Bernice was right there to explain it to him.

"I want to be a society vampire, you see," she declared calmly, and proceeded to tell him that having bobbed hair was an essential first step. She mentioned that she wanted his opinion because she had heard he was very particular when it came to judging girls.

Charley, who understood women's psychology about as well as he grasped the mindset of Buddhist monks deep in meditation, felt somewhat pleased with himself.

"So I've made up my mind," she went on, her voice getting a bit louder, "that early next week I'm heading down to the Sevier Hotel barbershop, taking the first chair, and getting my hair cut short." She hesitated when she noticed that the people around her had stopped talking and were listening in; but after a moment of confusion, Marjorie's training kicked in, and she addressed her remarks to everyone nearby. "Naturally I'm charging admission, but if you all come down and cheer me on, I'll give out tickets for the best seats."

There was a wave of appreciative laughter, and using it as cover, G. Reece Stoddard quickly leaned over and whispered close to her ear: "I'll take a box right now."

She looked into his eyes and smiled as though he had just said something remarkably clever.

"Do you believe in bobbed hair?" asked G. Reece in the same quiet voice.

"I think it's immoral," Bernice declared seriously. "But naturally, you have to either entertain people or nourish them or surprise them." Marjorie had borrowed this idea from Oscar Wilde. The comment was met with gentle laughter from the men and a succession of sharp, focused glances from the women. Then, as if she hadn't said anything clever or significant, Bernice turned back to Charley and whispered privately in his ear.

"I'd like to get your thoughts on a few different people. I have a feeling you're really good at reading people."

Charley felt a slight thrill and paid her a delicate compliment by accidentally knocking over her water.

Two hours later, Warren McIntyre stood passively in the stag line, absently watching the dancers and wondering where Marjorie had gone and who she was with, when an unrelated realization slowly began to dawn on him—he noticed that Bernice, Marjorie's cousin, had been cut in on several times during the past five minutes. He closed his eyes, opened them, and looked again. A few minutes earlier she had been dancing with a visiting boy, which was easily explained; a visiting boy wouldn't know any better. But now she was dancing with someone else, and there was Charley Paulson heading toward her with enthusiastic determination in his eyes. Strange—Charley rarely danced with more than three girls in an entire evening.

Warren was genuinely surprised when—after the exchange had taken place—the man he replaced turned out to be none other than G. Reece Stoddard himself. And G. Reece didn't seem at all happy about being replaced. The next time Bernice danced nearby, Warren watched her carefully. Yes, she was attractive, definitely attractive; and tonight her face appeared truly animated. She had that expression that no woman, no matter how skilled at acting, can fake convincingly—she looked like she was genuinely enjoying herself. He admired how she had styled her hair, wondering if it was hair product that made it shine like that. And that dress was flattering—a deep red that complemented her dark eyes and rich complexion. He recalled thinking she was pretty when she first arrived in town, before he had discovered that she was boring. What a shame she was boring—dull girls were impossible to tolerate—though she was certainly attractive.

His mind wandered back to Marjorie. This vanishing act would be just like all the others. When she showed up again, he would insist on knowing where she had been—only to be told firmly that it wasn't any of his concern. What a shame she felt so confident about him! She reveled in knowing that no other girl in town caught his attention; she dared him to develop feelings for Genevieve or Roberta.

Warren let out a sigh. Finding his way to Marjorie's heart was like navigating a maze. He glanced up and saw Bernice dancing once more with the boy from out of town. Without really thinking about it, he stepped away from the group of men standing along the wall and moved in her direction, then stopped. He told himself he was just being kind. He started walking toward her and suddenly bumped into G. Reece Stoddard.

"Excuse me," said Warren.

But G. Reece hadn't paused to offer an apology. He had once again cut in on Bernice.

That night at one o'clock, Marjorie stood in the hallway with one hand on the light switch, turning to take a final look at Bernice's sparkling eyes.

"So it worked?"

"Oh, Marjorie, yes!" cried Bernice.

"I saw you were having a wonderful time."

"I did! The only problem was that around midnight I ran out of things to say. I had to repeat myself—with different men, of course. I hope they won't compare notes."

"Men don't," said Marjorie, yawning, "and it wouldn't matter if they did—they'd think you were even more cunning."

She turned off the light, and as they began climbing the stairs, Bernice grabbed the banister gratefully. For the first time in her life, she had danced until she was exhausted.

"You see," said Marjorie at the top of the stairs, "when one man sees another man cut in, he thinks there must be something there. Well, we'll come up with some new material tomorrow. Good night."

"Good night."

As Bernice let down her hair, she reflected on the evening that had just passed. She had followed the instructions precisely. Even when Charley Paulson cut in for the eighth time, she had pretended to be delighted and had seemed both interested and flattered. She hadn't talked about the weather or Eau Claire or cars or her school, but had kept her conversation focused on me, you, and us.

But just a few minutes before she drifted off to sleep, a defiant thought was stirring lazily in her mind—when it came down to it, she was the one who had made it happen. Sure, Marjorie had taught her how to talk to people, but Marjorie got most of her conversation skills from books she'd read. Bernice had purchased the red dress, even though she'd never thought much of it until Marjorie pulled it from her trunk—and it was her own voice that had spoken those words, her own lips that had smiled, her own feet that had danced. Marjorie was a nice girl—conceited, though—lovely evening—nice guys—like Warren—Warren—Warren—what was his name—Warren—

She fell asleep.

Chapter 5

For Bernice, the following week opened her eyes to a whole new world. When she realized that people genuinely enjoyed her appearance and conversation, she began building real self-confidence for the first time. Naturally, she made plenty of blunders in the beginning. She had no idea, for example, that Draycott Deyo was preparing for the ministry; she didn't realize that he had asked her to dance because he believed she was a quiet, modest young woman. If she had understood these facts, she never would have greeted him with the phrase "Hello, Shell Shock!" and then launched into her bathtub story—"It requires an enormous amount of energy to style my hair during the summer months— there's just so much of it—so I always arrange my hair first, then apply powder to my face and put on my hat; after that I step into the bathtub, and get dressed once I'm finished. Don't you think that's the most sensible approach?"

Although Draycott Deyo was struggling with issues about baptism by full immersion and might have potentially made a connection, it has to be acknowledged that he didn't. He viewed women's bathing as an indecent topic, and shared with her some of his thoughts on the moral corruption of contemporary society.

However, to balance out that unfortunate incident, Bernice had achieved several notable victories. Young Otis Ormonde canceled a planned trip to the East Coast and chose instead to follow her around with the devoted loyalty of a puppy, much to his friends' entertainment and to G. Reece Stoddard's annoyance, since Otis completely spoiled several of Stoddard's afternoon visits with the sickeningly tender looks he directed at Bernice. Otis even shared with her the story about the two-by-four and the dressing room to demonstrate how terribly wrong he and everyone else had been in their initial assessment of her. Bernice brushed off that story with laughter, though she felt a small knot of uneasiness in her stomach.

Of all the things Bernice said in conversation, perhaps the most famous and widely praised was her comment about cutting her hair short.

"Oh, Bernice, when are you going to get your hair bobbed?"

"Maybe the day after tomorrow," she would reply, laughing. "Will you come and see me? Because I'm counting on you, you know."

"Will we? You know! But you better hurry up."

Bernice, whose hair-cutting plans were completely malicious, would laugh again.

"Pretty soon now. You'd be surprised."

But perhaps the most significant symbol of her success was the gray car belonging to the highly critical Warren McIntyre, parked every day in front of the Harvey house. Initially, the parlor-maid was clearly surprised when he asked to see Bernice instead of Marjorie; after a week of this, she told the cook that Miss Bernice had managed to steal Miss Marjorie's best boyfriend.

And Miss Bernice had succeeded. Maybe it started with Warren's desire to make Marjorie jealous; maybe it was the familiar yet unnoticed echo of Marjorie in Bernice's way of talking; maybe it was both of these things plus some genuine attraction as well. But somehow the group mind of the younger crowd figured out within a week that Marjorie's most dependable boyfriend had done a complete turnaround and was clearly pursuing Marjorie's houseguest with intensity. Everyone wanted to know how Marjorie would react. Warren called Bernice twice daily, sent her messages, and people often saw them together in his convertible, clearly absorbed in one of those intense, meaningful discussions about whether his feelings were real.

When people teased Marjorie about it, she just laughed it off. She said she was really happy that Warren had finally found someone who appreciated him. So the younger crowd laughed along with her and figured that Marjorie didn't mind, and they left it at that.

One afternoon, with just three days remaining of her visit, Bernice stood waiting in the hallway for Warren, who was taking her to a bridge party. She felt quite content and happy, and when Marjorie appeared next to her—also heading to the same party—and started casually fixing her hat in the mirror, Bernice was completely caught off guard by what was about to happen. Marjorie delivered her message with cold precision in just three sentences.

"You might as well forget about Warren," she said coldly.

"What?" Bernice was completely shocked.

"You might as well stop making a fool of yourself over Warren McIntyre. He doesn't care one bit about you."

For a tense moment they stared at each other— Marjorie contemptuous and distant; Bernice shocked, partly furious, partly frightened. Then two cars pulled up in front of the house and there was loud, chaotic honking. Both of them drew in sharp breaths, turned around, and rushed out together.

Throughout the entire bridge party, Bernice struggled unsuccessfully to control her growing anxiety. She had upset Marjorie, the most mysterious person of all. With completely pure and harmless motives, she had taken what belonged to Marjorie. She felt an immediate and terrible sense of guilt. Following the bridge game, when they gathered in a casual circle and everyone joined the conversation, the conflict slowly began to unfold. Little Otis Ormonde accidentally triggered it.

"When are you going back to kindergarten, Otis?" someone had asked.

"Me? The day Bernice gets her hair cut short."

33

"Then you're done with school," Marjorie said quickly. "She's just bluffing. I would have thought you'd figured that out by now."

"Is that really true?" Otis asked, shooting Bernice a disapproving look.

Bernice's ears burned as she struggled to come up with an effective comeback. Faced with this direct attack, her imagination was completely paralyzed.

"There are plenty of people who are just bluffing in this world," Marjorie continued in a pleasant tone. "I would think you'd be young enough to understand that, Otis."

"Well," said Otis, "maybe so. But wow! With a line like Bernice's——"

"Really?" Marjorie yawned. "What's her latest clever remark?"

No one appeared to have an answer. In reality, Bernice, having flirted with her muse's boyfriend, hadn't said anything worth remembering recently.

"Was that really all just an act?" asked Roberta curiously.

Bernice paused. She sensed that some kind of clever response was expected from her, but under her cousin's suddenly cold stare she found herself completely unable to speak.

"I don't know," she stalled.

"Splush!" said Marjorie. "Admit it!"

Bernice noticed that Warren had stopped fiddling with his ukulele and was now staring at her with a questioning look in his eyes.

"Oh, I don't know!" she said again with unwavering certainty. Her cheeks were flushed with color.

"Splush!" Marjorie said again.

"Come on, Bernice," Otis pressed her. "Tell her what's what." Bernice glanced around once more—she appeared unable to escape Warren's gaze.

"I like bobbed hair," she said quickly, as though he had posed a question to her, "and I plan to bob mine."

"When?" Marjorie demanded.

"Any time."

"No time like the present," suggested Roberta.

Otis jumped to his feet.

"Excellent!" he exclaimed. "We'll throw a summer bobbing party. The Sevier Hotel barbershop, I believe you mentioned."

In an instant, everyone jumped to their feet. Bernice's heart pounded violently.

"What?" she gasped.

Out of the group came Marjorie's voice, very clear and contemptuous.

"Don't worry—she'll back out!"

"Come on, Bernice!" shouted Otis, heading toward the door.

Four pairs of eyes—Warren's and Marjorie's—fixed on her, challenging her, daring her to act. For another moment she hesitated frantically.

"All right," she said quickly, "I don't care if I do."

What felt like an eternity of minutes passed as Bernice rode downtown through the late afternoon sitting next to Warren, with the others following closely behind in Roberta's car. She experienced all the feelings of Marie Antoinette heading to the guillotine in a cart. She vaguely wondered why she didn't call out that this was all a huge mistake. She could barely stop herself from grabbing her hair with both hands to shield it from the world that had suddenly turned against her. But she did nothing of the sort.

Not even thoughts of her mother could hold her back now. This was the ultimate test of her ability to be a good sport; her chance to earn the right to walk confidently among the most popular girls without anyone questioning her place there.

Warren remained moodily quiet, and when they arrived at the hotel he pulled up to the curb and gestured for Bernice to get out first. Roberta's car discharged a group of laughing people into the store, which displayed two large plate-glass windows facing the street.

Bernice stood at the edge of the sidewalk and stared at the sign reading "Sevier Barber-Shop." This place truly was like a guillotine, and the executioner was the first barber, who wore a white coat and smoked a cigarette while casually leaning against the first chair. He had to have heard about her; he had probably been waiting there all week, chain-smoking cigarettes next to that ominous, frequently discussed first chair. Would they put a blindfold on her? No, but they would wrap a white cloth around her neck to prevent any of her blood—ridiculous—her hair—from getting on her clothing.

"All right, Bernice," Warren said quickly.

With her chin held high, she walked across the sidewalk, pushed through the swinging screen door, and without even looking at the loud, rowdy group sitting on the waiting bench, approached the heavy-set barber.

"I want you to cut my hair short."

The first barber's mouth fell slightly open. His cigarette dropped to the floor.

"Huh?"

"My hair—cut it short!"

Without any more delays, Bernice sat down in the elevated chair. A man in the chair beside her shifted to his side and looked at her with an expression that was half soap suds, half astonishment. One barber jerked in surprise and ruined little Willy Schuneman's monthly trim. Mr. O'Reilly in the final chair groaned and cursed melodiously in old Gaelic as a razor nicked his cheek. Two shoe shiners stared with wide eyes and hurried toward her feet. No, Bernice didn't want a shoe shine.

Outside, someone walking by stopped and stared; a couple came over to join him; the noses of half a dozen small boys suddenly came to life, pressed flat against the glass; and fragments of conversation carried on the summer breeze floated in through the screen door.

"Look at that long hair on a kid!"

"Where did you get that stuff? That's a bearded lady he just finished shaving."

But Bernice saw nothing, heard nothing. Her only functioning sense told her that this man in the white coat had taken away one tortoise-shell comb and then another; that his fingers were struggling awkwardly with unfamiliar hairpins; that this hair, this magnificent hair of hers, was disappearing—she would never again experience its long sensual weight as it cascaded in dark-brown splendor down her back. For a moment she was close to falling apart, and then the image in front of her drifted automatically into her sight—Marjorie's mouth twisting into a slight mocking smile as if to say:

"Give up and get down! You tried to challenge me and I saw right through your empty threat. You can see that you don't stand a chance."

A final surge of energy welled up inside Bernice, and she clenched her fists beneath the white cloth, while her eyes narrowed in a strange way that Marjorie would mention to someone much later.

Twenty minutes later, the barber turned her chair around to face the mirror, and she winced at seeing the full scope of what had been done. Her hair no longer had curls and now hung in flat, lifeless chunks on either side of her suddenly ashen face. It was hideously ugly—she had known it would be hideously ugly. Her face's main appeal had been its Madonna-like innocence. Now that quality was gone and she looked—well, terribly ordinary—not theatrical; just absurd, like a Greenwich Village resident who had forgotten her glasses at home.

As she stepped down from the chair, she attempted to smile but failed completely. She caught sight of two girls exchanging looks, observed Marjorie's lips forming a thin, mocking curve, and noticed that Warren's eyes had suddenly turned ice-cold.

"You see,"—her words fell into an uncomfortable silence—"I've done it."

"Yes, you've—done it," Warren admitted.

"Do you like it?"

There was a lukewarm "Sure" from two or three voices, followed by another uncomfortable silence, and then Marjorie quickly turned toward Warren with snake-like focus.

"Would you mind giving me a ride to the dry cleaner's?" she asked. "I really need to pick up a dress before dinner. Roberta's heading straight home and she can take the others."

Warren gazed absent-mindedly at some distant point beyond the window. Then for a moment his eyes settled coldly on Bernice before shifting to Marjorie.

"I'd be happy to," he said slowly.

Chapter 6

Bernice didn't completely understand the shocking trap that had been laid for her until she caught her aunt's astonished look right before dinner.

"Why Bernice!"

"I've cut it short, Aunt Josephine."

"Why, child!"

"Do you like it?"

"Why Bernice!"

"I suppose I've shocked you."

"No, but what will Mrs. Deyo think tomorrow night? Bernice, you should have waited until after the Deyo's dance—you should have waited if you wanted to do that."

"It happened suddenly, Aunt Josephine. Besides, why should Mrs. Deyo care about it specifically?"

"Why child," exclaimed Mrs. Harvey, "in her presentation on 'The Foibles of the Younger Generation' that she delivered at the most recent Thursday Club meeting, she spent fifteen minutes discussing bobbed hair. It's what she despises most. And the dance is being held for you and Marjorie!"

"I'm sorry."

"Oh, Bernice, what will your mother say? She'll think I let you do it."

"I'm sorry."

Dinner was torture. She had quickly tried to use a curling iron and ended up burning her finger and a lot of her hair. She could tell that her aunt was both concerned and upset, and her uncle kept repeating, "Well, I'll be darned!" again and again in a wounded and slightly angry tone. Meanwhile, Marjorie sat very quietly, protected behind a subtle smile, a slightly mocking smile.

Somehow she managed to get through the evening. Three boys called; Marjorie vanished with one of them, and Bernice made a halfhearted, unsuccessful effort to entertain the other two—she sighed with relief as she walked up the stairs to her room at ten-thirty. What a day it had been!

When she had gotten undressed for the night, the door opened and Marjorie walked in.

"Bernice," she said, "I'm really sorry about the Deyo dance. I give you my word that I had completely forgotten about it."

"It's all right," said Bernice curtly. Standing in front of the mirror, she slowly ran her comb through her short hair.

"I'll take you downtown tomorrow," Marjorie continued, "and the hairdresser will fix it so you'll look great. I didn't think you'd actually go through with it. I'm really very sorry."

"Oh, it's all right!"

"Still, it's your last night, so I suppose it won't matter much."

Then Bernice flinched as Marjorie swept her own hair over her shoulders and started slowly twisting it into two long blonde braids until, wearing her cream-colored nightgown, she resembled a delicate portrait of some Saxon princess. Captivated, Bernice watched the braids take shape. Thick and lustrous, they moved beneath those nimble fingers like restless snakes—and all that remained for Bernice was this remnant, the curling iron, and a tomorrow filled with staring eyes. She could picture G. Reece Stoddard, who had feelings for her, putting on his Harvard airs and telling his dinner companion that Bernice shouldn't have been permitted to attend so many movies; she could envision Draycott Deyo sharing meaningful looks with his mother before making a point of being dutifully kind to her.

40

But perhaps by tomorrow Mrs. Deyo would have caught wind of the news; would send over a cold little message asking her not to come—and behind her back they would all snicker and realize that Marjorie had made her look ridiculous; that her opportunity for beauty had been destroyed by the spiteful impulse of a self-centered girl. She dropped into the chair in front of the mirror, chewing the inside of her cheek.

"I like it," she said, forcing herself to speak. "I think it will look good on me."

Marjorie smiled.

"It looks fine. For heaven's sake, don't let it worry you!"

"I won't."

"Good night Bernice."

But as the door closed, something broke inside Bernice. She jumped up energetically, clenching her fists, then quickly and silently walked over to her bed and pulled out her suitcase from underneath it. She threw in toiletries and a change of clothes. Then she turned to her trunk and rapidly emptied two drawers full of underwear and summer dresses into it. She worked quietly but with lethal efficiency, and within forty-five minutes her trunk was locked and secured with straps, and she was completely dressed in an attractive new travel outfit that Marjorie had helped her choose.

Settling into her chair at the desk, she composed a brief message to Mrs. Harvey, quickly explaining why she had decided to leave. After sealing and addressing the note, she placed it on her pillow. She checked the time on her watch. The train departed at one o'clock, and she realized that by walking to the Marborough Hotel just two blocks down the street, she could easily find a taxi.

Suddenly she took a sharp breath and a look flashed in her eyes that someone skilled at reading people might have loosely linked to the determined expression she had worn in the barber's chair—like it had evolved into something more. This was a completely new look for Bernice—and it would lead to consequences.

She quietly crept to the bureau, picked up an item that was lying there, and after turning off all the lights, stood still until her eyes adjusted to the darkness. Gently she pushed open the door to Marjorie's room. She could hear the calm, steady breathing of someone with a clear conscience sleeping peacefully.

She stood beside the bed now, moving with careful purpose and composure. She worked quickly. Leaning forward, she located one of Marjorie's braids, traced it upward with her fingers to where it began near the scalp, then held it loosely so the sleeping girl wouldn't feel any tugging as she brought the scissors down and cut through it. Clutching the severed braid, she held her breath. Marjorie had mumbled something while sleeping. Bernice skillfully cut off the second braid, hesitated briefly, then hurried quietly back to her own room without making a sound.

She went downstairs and opened the large front door, closing it carefully behind her. Feeling strangely happy and energetic, she stepped off the porch into the moonlight, carrying her heavy suitcase as casually as a shopping bag. After walking briskly for a minute, she realized that her left hand was still clutching the two blonde braids. She burst into unexpected laughter—she had to clamp her mouth shut to prevent herself from letting out a complete roar of laughter. She was now walking past Warren's house, and on a sudden impulse, she put down her luggage. Swinging the braids like a piece of rope, she hurled them at the wooden porch, where they hit with a soft thud. She laughed again, this time without holding back.

"Huh," she laughed hysterically. "Scalp the selfish thing!"

Then she grabbed her staircase and took off at a half-run down the moonlit street.

Blessing

Chapter 1

The Baltimore Station was sweltering and packed with people, forcing Lois to wait by the telegraph counter for what felt like endless, uncomfortable moments while a clerk with prominent front teeth counted and recounted a heavy-set woman's telegram, trying to figure out whether it contained the harmless forty-nine words or the problematic fifty-one.

Lois, while waiting, realized she wasn't completely certain about the address, so she pulled the letter from her bag and read through it once more.

"Darling," it began—"I understand and I'm happier than life ever intended me to be. If I could give you the things you've always connected with—but I can't Lois; we can't get married and we can't lose each other and let all this wonderful love end in nothing.

"Until your letter arrived, my dear, I had been sitting here in the dim light, wondering where I could go to ever forget you; perhaps abroad, to wander through Italy or Spain and lose myself in dreams that would ease the pain of losing you, where the crumbling ruins of ancient, more refined civilizations would reflect only the emptiness in my heart—and then your letter came."

"My dearest, most courageous girl, if you send me a telegram, I'll meet you in Wilmington—until then, I'll remain here simply waiting and hoping for every cherished dream of you to become reality."

"Howard."

She had read the letter countless times until she memorized every single word, but it continued to surprise her. Within its lines, she discovered subtle glimpses of the man who had written it—the combination of tenderness and melancholy in his dark eyes, the secretive, anxious energy she occasionally sensed when he spoke with her, his thoughtful sensuality that made her mind drift into a peaceful haze. Lois was nineteen and deeply romantic, inquisitive, and brave.

The large woman and the clerk reached an agreement on fifty words, so Lois picked up a blank form and composed her telegram. Her decision carried no hidden meanings or second thoughts about its finality.

It's simply fate, she thought to herself—it's just how things unfold in this cursed world. If fear has been the only thing preventing me from acting, then there won't be any more hesitation. So we'll allow events to unfold naturally and never feel regret about it.

The clerk looked over her telegram:

"Arrived in Baltimore today, spending the day with my brother. Meet me in Wilmington at three P.M. on Wednesday. Love"

"Lois."

"Fifty-four cents," the clerk said with admiration.

And never feel regret—Lois thought—and never feel regret——

Chapter 2

Trees filter light onto dappled grass. Trees stand like tall, graceful ladies with feather fans flirting playfully with the unsightly monastery roof. Trees resemble butlers, bowing politely over peaceful walkways and paths. Trees, trees spread across the hills on both sides and scatter in clusters and rows and forests throughout eastern Maryland, forming delicate lace along the edges of numerous golden fields, creating dark solid backdrops for flowering bushes or wild climbing gardens.

Some of the trees were vibrant and youthful, but the monastery trees were older than the monastery itself, which by genuine monastic standards wasn't very old at all. And actually, it wasn't technically called a monastery, but rather a seminary; however it will be referred to as a monastery here despite its Victorian architecture or its Edward VII additions, or even its Woodrow Wilson-era, patented, century-lasting roofing.

Out behind stood the farm where half a dozen lay brothers worked up a sweat as they moved with lethal efficiency through the vegetable gardens. To the left, beyond a line of elm trees, lay an improvised baseball field where three novices were getting struck out by a fourth player, accompanied by lots of running around, heavy breathing, and panting. And out front, as a deep, rich bell rang out the half-hour, a crowd of black-robed figures scattered like human leaves across the crisscrossing walkways beneath the graceful trees.

Some of these dark-skinned students were quite elderly, their faces lined with wrinkles like the initial waves spreading across a disturbed pond. Then there were a number of middle-aged students whose silhouettes, when seen from the side in their form-fitting dresses, were starting to show subtle signs of asymmetry. These women carried heavy books by Thomas Aquinas and Henry James and Cardinal Mercier and Immanuel Kant, along with numerous thick notebooks crammed with lecture notes.

But the majority were the young leaves; fair-haired nineteen-year-old boys with very serious, earnest expressions; men in their late twenties with sharp self-confidence gained from teaching in the real world for five years—several hundred of them, coming from cities and towns and rural areas throughout Maryland and Pennsylvania and Virginia and West Virginia and Delaware.

There were many Americans and some Irish and some tough Irish and a few French, and several Italians and Poles, and they walked casually arm in arm with each other in pairs and groups of three or in long lines, almost all marked by their firm mouths and strong chins—for this was the Society of Jesus, established in Spain five centuries earlier by a determined soldier who prepared men to defend a fortress or navigate a drawing room, deliver a sermon or draft a treaty, and accomplish it without debate . . .

Lois stepped off a bus into the bright sunlight near the outer gate. She was nineteen years old, with blonde hair and eyes that people politely avoided describing as green. When gifted men spotted her on a streetcar, they would secretly pull out small pencil stubs and envelope backs, attempting to capture her profile or the way her eyebrows enhanced her eyes. Afterward, they would examine their sketches and typically tear them up with puzzled sighs.

Although Lois was dressed quite stylishly in an expensive and suitable traveling outfit, she didn't stop to brush off the dust that had settled on her clothing, but instead hurried up the main walkway while casting inquisitive looks from side to side. Her expression was filled with eagerness and anticipation, though she didn't have that radiant look that young women display when they arrive for a Senior Prom at Princeton or Yale; however, since there were no senior proms at this place, perhaps that wasn't important.

She wondered what he would look like and whether she might recognize him from his photograph. In the photo that hung above her mother's dresser at home, he appeared very young and gaunt, looking rather pitiful with only a well-developed mouth and an ill-fitting seminary student's robe to indicate that he had already made a life-changing decision. Naturally, he had been only nineteen at that time, and now he was thirty-six—he didn't look like that anymore; in recent photographs he appeared much broader and his hair had thinned somewhat—but the image of her brother she had always kept was that of the large picture. And so she had always felt a little sorry for him. What kind of life was that for a man! Seventeen years of training and he still wasn't even a priest yet—wouldn't be for another year.

Lois sensed that this whole situation could turn quite serious if she allowed it to happen. However, she was determined to put on her brightest, most cheerful act—the same performance she could deliver even when she had a terrible headache, when her mother was having an emotional crisis, or when she felt especially dreamy, inquisitive, and bold. Her brother clearly needed someone to lift his spirits, and she was going to brighten his mood whether he wanted it or not.

As she approached the large, welcoming front door, she noticed a man suddenly separate from a group and rush toward her, lifting the hem of his robe as he ran. She observed that he was smiling, and he appeared very tall and dependable. She paused and waited, aware that her heart was pounding faster than usual.

"Lois!" he shouted, and within seconds she was in his arms. She began trembling suddenly.

"Lois!" he called out again, "this is incredible! I can't express to you, Lois, how much I've been anticipating this moment. Lois, you're absolutely beautiful!"

Lois gasped.

His voice, while controlled, pulsed with energy and that strange kind of encompassing presence she had believed only she in the family had.

"I'm really glad too, Keith."

She blushed, but not unhappily, at this first use of his name.

"Lois—Lois—Lois," he said again with amazement. "Dear, we'll step inside here for a moment, because I want you to meet the rector, and then we'll take a walk around. I have so many things I want to discuss with you."

His voice grew more serious. "How's mother?"

She looked at him for a moment and then said something she hadn't meant to say at all, exactly the kind of thing she had promised herself she wouldn't say.

"Oh, Keith—she's—she's getting worse all the time, in every way."

He nodded slowly as if he understood.

"Nervous, well—you can tell me about that later. Now——"

She was in a small study with a large desk, speaking to a little, cheerful, white-haired priest who held her hand for several seconds.

"So this is Lois!"

He spoke as though he had known about her for years.

He begged her to take a seat.

Two other priests arrived with enthusiasm and shook hands with her, addressing her as "Kieth's little sister," which she discovered didn't bother her at all.

How confident they appeared; she had anticipated some timidity, or at least a bit of restraint. Several jokes that she couldn't understand seemed to amuse everyone greatly, and the little Father Rector called the three of them "dim old monks," which she found charming, since obviously they weren't monks at all. She had a quick sense that they were particularly fond of Kieth—the Father Rector had addressed him as "Kieth" and one of the others had kept his hand on Kieth's shoulder throughout their entire conversation. Then she found herself shaking hands once more and agreeing to return later for some ice-cream, and smiling and smiling and feeling ridiculously happy . . . she convinced herself that her joy came from seeing how thrilled Kieth was to show her off.

Then she and Kieth walked together along a path, arm in arm, while he told her what an absolute treasure the Father Rector was.

"Lois," he stopped abruptly, "I need to tell you before we continue how much it means to me that you came up here. I think it was—really thoughtful of you. I know what a wonderful time you've been having."

Lois gasped. She hadn't been ready for this. When she first came up with the plan to make the sweltering trip down to Baltimore, spend the night with a friend, and then come out to visit her brother, she had felt somewhat self-righteously good about herself, hoping he wouldn't be stuffy or bitter about her not having visited before—but walking here with him beneath the trees felt like such a small thing, and unexpectedly a joyful thing.

"Why, Keith," she said quickly, "you know I couldn't have waited a day longer. I saw you when I was five, but of course I didn't remember, and how could I have gone on without practically ever having seen my only brother?"

"That was really sweet of you, Lois," he said again.

Lois felt her cheeks grow warm—he certainly had character.

"I want you to tell me everything about yourself," he said after a moment of silence. "Naturally, I have a basic understanding of what you and mother were doing in Europe during those fourteen years, and then we were all so concerned, Lois, when you came down with pneumonia and couldn't travel back with mother—let me think, that was two years ago—and then, well, I've noticed your name mentioned in the newspapers, but it's all been so inadequate. I haven't really known you, Lois."

She found herself studying his character the same way she examined every man she encountered. She wondered whether the sense of closeness he created came from how often he repeated her name. He spoke it as though he cherished the sound, as though it held some special significance for him.

"Then you were at school," he continued.

"Yes, at Farmington. Mother wanted me to go to a convent—but I didn't want to."

She glanced at him sideways to see if this would upset him.

But he only nodded slowly.

"Had enough convents abroad, eh?"

"Yes—and Keith, convents are different there anyway. Here even in the nicest ones there are so many common girls."

He nodded again.

"Yes," he agreed, "I suppose there are, and I understand how you feel about it. It bothered me here at first, Lois, though I wouldn't admit that to anyone but you; we're both quite sensitive, you and I, to things like this."

"You mean the men here?"

"Yes, some of them were certainly decent people, the kind of men I'd always associated with, but there were others; a man named Regan, for example—I couldn't stand the guy, and now he's one of my closest friends. He's an amazing person, Lois; you'll meet him later. The kind of man you'd want by your side in a tough situation."

Lois was thinking that Keith was the kind of man she would want by her side in a fight.

"How did you—how did you first end up doing it?" she asked, somewhat shyly, "coming here, I mean. Of course mother told me the story about the Pullman car."

"Oh, that——" He looked quite irritated.

"Tell me that. I'd like to hear you tell it."

"Oh, it's nothing more than what you probably already know. It was evening and I had been riding all day, thinking about—about a hundred different things, Lois, when suddenly I sensed that someone was sitting across from me. I felt that this person had been there for quite some time, and I had this vague impression that he was another traveler. All at once he leaned toward me and I heard a voice say: 'I want you to become a priest, that's what I want.' Well, I jumped up and shouted, 'Oh, my God, not that!'—I made a complete fool of myself in front of about twenty people; you see, there wasn't anyone sitting there at all. A week later I went to the Jesuit College in Philadelphia and crawled up the final flight of stairs to the rector's office on my hands and knees."

There was another silence, and Lois noticed that her brother's eyes had a distant expression, as if he was gazing blindly across the sunlit fields. She felt moved by the changes in his voice and the sudden quiet that seemed to surround him when he stopped talking.

She realized now that his eyes were made of the same material as hers, just without the green, and that his mouth was actually much softer than it appeared in the photograph—or perhaps his face had recently matured to match it? He was starting to lose some hair right at the crown of his head. She wondered if that came from wearing a hat so often. It seemed terrible for a man to go bald with no one there to worry about it.

"Were you devout when you were young, Keith?" she asked. "You understand what I'm getting at. Were you a believer? If you don't mind me asking such personal questions."

"Yes," he said, his gaze still distant—and she realized that his deep preoccupation was just as much a part of who he was as his focused attention. "Yes, I suppose I was, when I was—sober."

Lois felt a small shiver of excitement.

"Did you drink?"

He nodded.

"I was about to mess everything up badly." He smiled and, looking at her with his gray eyes, changed the topic.

"Child, tell me about mother. I know things have been really difficult for you there recently. I know you've had to give up a lot and endure so much, and I want you to understand how admirable I think you are. I feel, Lois, that you're essentially filling the role of both of us there."

Lois quickly realized how little she had actually given up; how recently she had been constantly avoiding her anxious, semi-invalid mother.

"Young people shouldn't have to sacrifice themselves for older generations, Keith," she said with conviction.

"I know," he sighed, "and you shouldn't have to carry this burden, child. I wish I could be there to help you."

She noticed how quickly he had twisted her comment around, and in that moment she realized what quality he radiated. He was charming. Her mind wandered off on a tangent, and then she interrupted the quiet with a strange observation.

"Sweetness is hard," she said suddenly.

"What?"

"Nothing," she said, flustered and confused. "I didn't mean to say that out loud. I was just thinking about something—about a conversation I had with a man named Freddy Kebble."

"Maury Kebble's brother?"

"Yes," she said, somewhat surprised to learn that he had known Maury Kebble. Still, there was nothing unusual about it. "Well, he and I were discussing sweetness a few weeks ago. Oh, I don't know—I mentioned that a man named Howard—that a man I knew was sweet, and he disagreed with me, and we started talking about what sweetness in a man actually was: He kept insisting I meant some kind of mushy softness, but I knew I didn't—though I couldn't figure out exactly how to express it. I understand now. I meant precisely the opposite. I think true sweetness is actually a kind of toughness—and strength."

Keith nodded.

"I understand what you're saying. I've known elderly priests who experienced that."

"I'm talking about young men," she said with a defiant tone.

They had arrived at the baseball diamond, which was now empty, and after directing her to a wooden bench, he stretched out completely on the grass.

"Are these young men happy here, Kieth?"

"Don't they look happy, Lois?"

"I suppose so, but those young ones, those two we just passed—have they—are they——?"

"Are they signed up?" he laughed. "No, but they will be next month."

"Permanently?"

"Yes—unless they have a mental or physical breakdown. Naturally, in a field like ours, many people drop out."

"But what about those boys? Are they giving up good opportunities elsewhere—just like you did?"

He nodded.

"Some of them."

"But Keith, they don't know what they're doing. They haven't had any experience of what they're missing."

"No, I suppose not."

"It doesn't seem fair. Life has simply frightened them from the start. Do they all arrive here so young?"

"No, some of them have lived rough lives and been through a lot—Regan, for example."

"I think that type would be better," she said thoughtfully, "men who had experienced life."

"No," Keith said earnestly, "I'm not convinced that wandering around aimlessly gives a person the kind of experience they can share with others. Some of the most open-minded people I've known have been completely strict with themselves. And former libertines who've changed their ways are famously intolerant. Don't you think so, Lois?"

She nodded, still lost in thought, and he continued:

"It seems to me that when one weak person reaches out to another, they don't really want help; they're looking for someone to share their guilt with, Lois. After you were born, when mother started getting anxious, she would go cry with a woman named Mrs. Comstock. God, it used to make me shudder. She claimed it gave her comfort, poor mother. No, I don't believe you need to expose yourself to help others. True help comes from someone stronger than you, someone you look up to. And their compassion means more because it's not personal."

"But people crave human understanding," Lois protested. "They need to sense that the other person has faced similar struggles."

"Lois, deep down they want to believe that the other person has shown weakness. That's what they really mean when they talk about being human."

"Here in this old monastery, Lois," he went on with a smile, "they work to strip away all that self-pity and pride in our own desires right from the beginning. They have us scrubbing floors—among other tasks. It's similar to that concept of saving your life by losing it. You understand, we believe that the less human a person becomes, in your understanding of what human means, the better he can serve humanity. We follow this principle completely. When one of us passes away, his family cannot even claim him. He's laid to rest here beneath a simple wooden cross alongside a thousand others."

His tone shifted abruptly and he gazed at her with a brilliant gleam in his gray eyes.

"But deep down in a man's heart there are some things he can't get rid of—and one of them is that I'm deeply in love with my little sister."

With a sudden impulse, she knelt beside him in the grass and leaned over to kiss his forehead.

"You're tough, Keith," she said, "and I love you for it— and you're sweet."

Chapter 3

Back in the reception room, Lois encountered half a dozen more of Keith's close friends; among them was a young man named Jarvis, somewhat pale and fragile in appearance, who she realized must be the grandson of old Mrs. Jarvis from back home, and she found herself mentally contrasting this austere figure with a pair of his wild and unruly uncles.

And there was Regan with a scarred face and piercing, intense eyes that tracked her movements around the room and frequently settled on Kieth with something that closely resembled worship. She understood then what Kieth had meant when he said Regan was "a good man to have with you in a fight."

He was the missionary type, she thought vaguely—China or something.

"I want Keith's sister to show us what the shimmy is," demanded one young man with a broad grin.

Lois laughed.

"I'm afraid the Father Rector would send me packing through the gate. Besides, I'm not an expert."

"I'm certain it wouldn't be good for Jimmy's soul anyway," Keith said seriously. "He tends to dwell on things like dance crazes. They had just begun doing the—maxixe, wasn't that right, Jimmy?—when he entered the monastery, and it troubled him throughout his entire first year. You would catch him while he was peeling potatoes, wrapping his arm around the bucket and making unholy movements with his feet."

There was a general laugh that Lois joined in on.

"An elderly woman who attends Mass here sent Keith this ice cream," Jarvis whispered while everyone was laughing, "because she heard you were coming. It's quite good, isn't it?"

There were tears welling up in Lois' eyes.

Chapter 4

Then thirty minutes later in the chapel, everything suddenly went terribly wrong. It had been several years since Lois had attended Benediction, and initially she felt excited by the shining monstrance with its central white focal point, the atmosphere thick and dense with incense, and the sunlight streaming through the stained-glass window of St. Francis Xavier above, casting warm red patterns on the cassock of the man seated in front of her, but when the opening notes of the "O salutaris hostia" began, a profound heaviness seemed to settle over her spirit. Kieth sat to her right and young Jarvis to her left, and she cast nervous glances at both of them.

"What's wrong with me?" she thought with frustration.

She looked once more. Was there a particular coldness in both of their faces that she hadn't observed before—a paleness around their mouths and a strange, fixed look in their eyes? She trembled slightly: they resembled corpses.

She felt her soul suddenly pull away from Kieth's. This was her brother—this strange, unnatural person. She caught herself starting to let out a small laugh.

"What's wrong with me?"

She ran her hand across her eyes and the heaviness grew stronger. The incense made her feel nauseous and a wandering, harsh note from one of the male singers in the choir scraped against her ear like the screech of chalk on a blackboard. She shifted restlessly, and lifting her hand to her hair, she touched her forehead and discovered it was damp with perspiration.

"It's hot in here, extremely hot."

Again she held back a quiet laugh, but then in a moment the heaviness in her chest suddenly transformed into cold fear. It was that candle on the altar. Something was completely wrong—terribly wrong. Why couldn't anyone else see it? There was something within it. There was something emerging from it, beginning to take form and shape above it.

She struggled to suppress her growing panic, convincing herself it had to be the wick. When a wick wasn't properly aligned, candles would behave strangely—but nothing like this! With impossible speed, a power was building inside her, an immense, absorbing energy that pulled from every sensation, every part of her mind, and as it rushed through her she experienced a massive, frightened revulsion. She pulled her arms tight against her body, away from Kieth and Jarvis.

Something about that candle... she was leaning forward—in another moment she felt she would move toward it—didn't anyone see it?... anyone?

"Ugh!"

She sensed an empty space next to her and something made her aware that Jarvis had drawn in a sharp breath and dropped into his seat abruptly . . . then she found herself on her knees and as the blazing monstrance was slowly carried away from the altar in the priest's hands, she heard a tremendous rushing sound in her ears—the crashing of the bells struck like hammer blows . . . and then in a moment that felt like eternity a powerful flood swept over her heart—there was a roaring there and a beating like crashing waves . . .

She was calling, felt herself calling for Kieth, her lips forming the words that wouldn't come:

"Keith! Oh, my God! Keith!"

Suddenly she became aware of a new presence, something outside herself, in front of her, complete and revealed in warm red patterns. Then she understood. It was the window of St. Francis Xavier. Her mind seized upon it, held onto it desperately, and she felt herself calling again without end, helplessly—Kieth—Kieth!

Then out of a great stillness came a voice:

"Blessed be God."

With a gradual rumble, the response echoed heavily throughout the chapel:

"Blessed be God."

The words immediately resonated in her heart; the incense hung mystically and sweetly peaceful in the air, and the candle on the altar was extinguished.

"Blessed be His Holy Name."

"Blessed be His Holy Name."

Everything became a blur of swirling mist. With a sound that was part gasp, part cry, she swayed on her feet and stumbled backward into Kieth's arms, which he had quickly extended to catch her.

Chapter 5

"Lie still, child."

She closed her eyes again. She was lying on the grass outside, her head resting on Kieth's arm, while Regan gently dabbed her forehead with a cold towel.

"I'm all right," she said quietly.

"I know, but just stay still for another minute. It was too hot in there. Jarvis felt it as well."

She laughed as Regan once again gently dabbed her with the towel.

"I'm all right," she said again.

But even though a warm sense of peace was settling over her mind and heart, she felt strangely broken and humbled, as if someone had exposed her naked soul and mocked it.

Chapter 6

Half an hour later, she walked down the long central path toward the gate, leaning on Keith's arm.

"It's been such a short afternoon," he sighed, "and I'm so sorry you were sick, Lois."

"Keith, I'm feeling fine now, really; I wish you wouldn't worry."

"Poor kid. I didn't realize that Benediction would be such a long service for you after your hot trip out here and everything."

She laughed cheerfully.

"I suppose the truth is I'm not very accustomed to Benediction. Mass is as far as my religious efforts go."

She paused and then continued quickly:

"I don't want to shock you, Keith, but I can't tell you how inconvenient being a Catholic is. It really doesn't seem relevant anymore. When it comes to morals, some of the most reckless guys I know are Catholics. And the smartest guys—I mean the ones who think deeply and read extensively, don't seem to believe in much of anything anymore."

"Tell me about it. The bus won't be here for another half-hour."

They sat down on a bench beside the path.

"Take Gerald Carter, for example—he's published a novel. He absolutely explodes with laughter whenever anyone brings up immortality. And then there's Howa—well, another man I've gotten to know well recently, who was Phi Beta Kappa at Harvard—he says that no intelligent person can believe in Supernatural Christianity. Though he does say Christ was a great socialist. Am I shocking you?"

She stopped speaking abruptly.

Keith smiled.

"You can't shock a monk. He's a professional shock-absorber."

"Well," she went on, "that's basically everything. It feels so—so restrictive. Take church schools, for example. There's more freedom regarding things that Catholic people can't understand—like birth control."

Keith winced, almost imperceptibly, but Lois saw it.

"Oh," she said quickly, "everyone talks about everything these days."

"It's probably better that way."

"Oh, yes, much better. Well, that's all, Keith. I just wanted to tell you why I'm a little—lukewarm, at present."

"I'm not surprised, Lois. I understand this better than you realize. We all experience these difficult periods. But I know everything will work out fine, child. We have that gift of faith, you and I, that will help us get through the tough times."

He stood up as he spoke, and they began walking down the path again.

"I want you to pray for me sometimes, Lois. I think your prayers would be exactly what I need. Because we've grown very close during these past few hours, I believe."

Her eyes suddenly began to sparkle.

"Oh we have, we have!" she exclaimed. "I feel closer to you right now than to anyone else in the world."

He came to an abrupt halt and pointed toward the edge of the trail.

"We might—just a minute——"

It was a pietà, a life-size statue of the Blessed Virgin positioned within a semicircular arrangement of rocks.

Feeling somewhat embarrassed, she knelt down next to him and tried unsuccessfully to pray.

She was only halfway finished when he stood up. He took hold of her arm once more.

"I wanted to thank Her for letting us have this day together," he said simply.

Lois felt a sudden tightness in her throat and wanted to tell him how much it had meant to her as well. However, she couldn't find the right words.

"I'll always remember this," he continued, his voice shaking slightly——"this summer day with you. It's been exactly what I hoped for. You're exactly what I hoped for, Lois."

"I'm really glad, Keith."

"You see, when you were little they kept sending me photographs of you, first as a baby and then as a child wearing socks playing on the beach with a bucket and shovel, and then suddenly as a thoughtful little girl with curious, innocent eyes—and I used to create dreams about you. A man needs something alive to hold onto. I think, Lois, it was your pure little spirit I tried to keep close to me—even when life was at its most chaotic and every rational concept of

God seemed like complete nonsense, and passion and love and countless other things approached me and said: 'Look at me! See, I'm Life. You're turning your back on it!' Throughout that entire darkness, Lois, I could always see your innocent soul dancing ahead of me, so delicate and bright and beautiful."

Lois was crying quietly. They had arrived at the gate and she leaned her elbow against it while wiping at her eyes frantically.

"And then later, child, when you were sick I knelt all night long and begged God to let you live—because I realized then that I wanted more; He had shown me how to want more. I wanted to know that you were moving and breathing in the same world as me. I could see you growing up, that pure innocence of yours transforming into a flame and burning bright to give light to other struggling souls. And then I wanted someday to hold your children on my knee and hear them call the grumpy old monk Uncle Keith."

He appeared to be laughing as he spoke.

"Oh, Lois, Lois, I was asking God for so much more back then. I wanted the letters you would write to me and the seat I would have at your table. I wanted so very much, dear Lois."

"You have me, Keith," she cried, "you know that, tell me you know it. Oh, I'm behaving like a child but I didn't expect you to act this way, and I—oh, Keith—Keith——"

He took her hand and gently patted it.

"Here's the bus. You'll come again, won't you?"

She placed her hands on his cheeks, and drawing his head down, pressed her tear-wet face against his.

"Oh, Keith, brother, someday I'll tell you something."

He helped her climb aboard, watched as she pulled out her handkerchief and gave him a courageous smile, while the driver cracked his whip and the bus began to move away. Then a dense cloud of dust swirled up around the vehicle and she had disappeared.

For a few minutes he stood there on the road with his hand on the gate-post, his lips slightly parted in a smile.

"Lois," he said out loud with a kind of amazement, "Lois, Lois."

Later, some novices walking by noticed him kneeling in front of the pietà, and when they returned after some time, they found him still in the same position. He remained there until dusk fell and the graceful trees began rustling noisily above and the crickets started their chorus of song in the darkening grass.

Chapter 7

The first clerk in the telegraph booth at the Baltimore Station whistled through his protruding front teeth to the second clerk:

"S'matter?"

"Look at that girl—no, the attractive one with the large black spots on her veil. Too late—she's disappeared. You missed something."

"What about her?"

"Nothing. Except she's really good-looking. She came in here yesterday and sent a telegram to some guy to meet her somewhere. Then a minute ago she walked in with a telegram all written out and was standing there about to hand it to me when she changed her mind or something and suddenly tore it up."

"Hm."

The first clerk walked around the counter and picked up the two pieces of paper from the floor, casually putting them back together. The second clerk read over his shoulder and automatically counted the words as he read. There were exactly thirteen.

"This is like a permanent farewell. I would recommend Italy."

"Lois."

"Tore it up, eh?" said the second clerk.

Dalrymple Goes Wrong

Chapter 1

In the future, an educational genius will write a book to be given to every young man when he becomes disillusioned. This work will have the character of Montaigne's essays and Samuel Butler's notebooks—and a touch of Tolstoy and Marcus Aurelius. It will be neither uplifting nor enjoyable but will include many passages of remarkable humor. Since brilliant minds never truly believe anything until they've lived through it, its worth will be entirely relative . . . everyone over thirty will describe it as "depressing."

This introduction is part of the story of a young man who lived, just as you and I do, before the book.

Chapter 2

The generation that included Bryan Dalyrimple emerged from their teenage years to tremendous fanfare and celebration. Bryan became the hero of an incident involving a Lewis gun and a nine-day adventure behind retreating German forces, so either extraordinary luck or overwhelming emotion earned him a collection of medals, and when he returned to the United States he was informed that only General Pershing and Sergeant York ranked higher in importance. This turned out to be quite enjoyable. His state's governor, a visiting congressman, and a committee of local citizens greeted him with huge grins and enthusiastic "By God, Sirs" at the Hoboken pier; newspaper reporters and photographers approached him saying "would you mind" and "if you could just"; and back in his hometown there were elderly women whose eyes welled up with tears as they spoke with him, and young women who hadn't paid him much attention since his father's business collapsed in nineteen-twelve.

But when the shouting died down, he came to understand that for an entire month he had been staying as a guest in the mayor's house, that he possessed only fourteen dollars to his name, and that "the name that will live forever in the annals and legends of this State" was already existing there in complete silence and anonymity.

One morning he stayed in bed late and just outside his door he heard the upstairs maid talking to the cook. The upstairs maid said that Mrs. Hawkins, the mayor's wife, had been trying for a week to hint that Dalyrimple should leave the house. He left at eleven o'clock in unbearable confusion, asking that his trunk be sent to Mrs. Beebe's boarding house.

Dalyrimple was twenty-three years old and had never held a job. His father had provided him with two years of education at the State University before dying around the time of his son's nine-day celebration, leaving behind some mid-Victorian furniture and a small bundle of folded papers that proved to be unpaid grocery bills. Young Dalyrimple possessed sharp gray eyes, an intellect that impressed the army's psychological evaluators, a talent for having already read whatever book or material was being discussed, and the ability to stay calm under pressure. However, these qualities couldn't prevent him from letting out one last, reluctant sigh when he understood that he needed to find employment immediately.

It was early afternoon when he entered Theron G. Macy's office, the man who owned the biggest wholesale grocery business in the city. Plump and successful, sporting a friendly yet completely serious expression, Theron G. Macy welcomed him with enthusiasm.

"Well—how are you doing, Bryan? What's on your mind?"

To Dalyrimple, struggling with his confession, his own words sounded like the pleading whine of an Arab beggar asking for charity when he finally spoke.

"Why—this matter of employment." ("This matter of employment" seemed somehow more dignified than simply "a job.")

"A job?" A barely noticeable shift crossed Mr. Macy's face.

"You see, Mr. Macy," Dalyrimple went on, "I feel like I'm wasting time. I want to get started on something. I had several opportunities about a month ago, but they all seem to have disappeared."

"Let's see," interrupted Mr. Macy. "What were they?"

"Well, right at the beginning the governor mentioned something about an opening on his staff. I was kind of hoping for that position for a while, but I heard he gave it to Allen Gregg, you know, G. P. Gregg's son. He sort of forgot what he told me—just making conversation, I suppose."

"You should push those things."

"Then there was that engineering expedition, but they decided they needed someone who understood hydraulics, so they couldn't take me unless I paid for my own trip."

"You only spent one year at the university?"

"Two. But I didn't take any science or mathematics. Well, the day the battalion paraded, Mr. Peter Jordan mentioned something about an opening in his store. I went over there today and discovered he was talking about a kind of floor supervisor position—and then you mentioned something one day"—he stopped and waited for the older man to respond, but seeing only a slight grimace, he went on—"about a job, so I thought I'd come and talk to you."

"There was an opening," Mr. Macy admitted with reluctance, "but we've already filled it since then." He cleared his throat once more. "You've been waiting for quite some time."

"Yes, I suppose I did. Everyone told me there was no rush—and I'd received these different offers."

Mr. Macy gave a speech about current opportunities, but Dalrymple's mind wandered completely and missed everything he said.

"Do you have any business experience?"

"I spent two summers working as a rider on a ranch."

"Oh, well," Mr. Macy dismissed this smoothly, and then went on: "What do you think you're worth?"

"I don't know."

"Well, Bryan, I'm telling you, I'm willing to make an exception and give you a chance."

Dalyrimple nodded.

"Your salary won't be much. You'll start by learning the inventory. Then you'll work in the office for a while. After that, you'll go on the road. When could you start?"

"How about tomorrow?"

"All right. Report to Mr. Hanson in the stockroom. He'll get you started."

He kept staring at Dalyrimple without looking away until Dalyrimple understood that their meeting had come to an end and stood up clumsily.

"Well, Mr. Macy, I'm certainly very grateful."

"That's all right. Glad to help you, Bryan."

After a moment of uncertainty, Dalyrimple found himself in the hallway. His forehead was covered with sweat, even though the room hadn't been warm.

"Why the hell did I thank that bastard?" he muttered.

Chapter 3

The next morning, Mr. Hanson coldly informed him that he would need to punch the time clock at seven every morning, and handed him over to a coworker named Charley Moore for training.

Charley was twenty-six, carrying that subtle hint of weakness around him that people often mistake for something sinister. You didn't need to be a trained psychologist to see that he had slipped into self-indulgence and laziness just as carelessly as he had stumbled into existence, and would eventually stumble out of it. His complexion was pale and his clothing reeked of cigarette smoke; he had a fondness for burlesque theaters, pool halls, and Robert Service's poetry, and spent his time either reminiscing about his most recent affair or anticipating his next one. During his younger years he had favored flashy neckties, but now his taste seemed to have dulled, much like his energy, showing itself in pale purple four-in-hand ties and nondescript gray shirt collars. Charley was halfheartedly fighting that inevitable battle against mental, moral, and physical exhaustion that constantly plays out among those barely clinging to middle-class status.

The first morning, he stretched out on a row of cereal boxes and carefully reviewed the limitations of the Theron G. Macy Company.

"It's a cheap organization. My God! Look at what they give me. I'm quitting in a couple of months. Hell! Why would I stay with this bunch!"

The Charley Moores are always planning to change jobs next month. They actually do switch positions once or twice during their careers, and afterward they spend their time comparing their previous job with their current one, endlessly criticizing the new position.

"What do you get?" Dalrymple asked with curiosity.

"Me? I get sixty." This was said rather defiantly.

"Did you start at sixty?"

"Me? No, I started when I was thirty-five. He told me he'd put me on the road after I learned the inventory. That's what he tells everyone."

"How long have you been here?" asked Dalyrimple with a sinking sensation.

"Me? Four years. This is my last year, too, you can count on it."

Dalyrimple found the store detective's presence irritating, much like how he felt about the time-clock, and he encountered him almost right away because of the no-smoking policy. This rule really bothered him. He was used to having three or four cigarettes during his morning routine, and after going without them for three days, he followed Charley Moore along a roundabout path up some back stairs to a small balcony where they could smoke in peace. However, this arrangement didn't last long. During his second week on the job, the detective caught him in a corner of the stairwell as he was coming back down and sternly warned him that if it happened again, he'd be reported to Mr. Macy. Dalyrimple felt like a student who'd been caught breaking the rules.

Disturbing realities came to light. There were "cave-dwellers" working in the basement who had been there for ten or fifteen years earning sixty dollars monthly, spending their days rolling barrels and hauling boxes through humid, concrete-lined hallways, trapped in that reverberating twilight from seven in the morning until five-thirty in the evening and, just like him, forced to stay until nine at night several times each month.

At the end of a month he stood in line and received forty dollars. He pawned a cigarette case and a pair of binoculars and managed to survive—to eat, sleep, and smoke. It was, however, a close call; since the methods and strategies of saving money were completely foreign to him and the second month brought no raise, he expressed his concern.

"If you have some influence with old Macy, he might give you a raise," Charley replied in a discouraging tone. "But he didn't give me a raise until I'd been working here for almost two years."

"I have to make a living," Dalyrimple said plainly. "I could earn more money working as a laborer for the railroad, but honestly, I want to feel like I'm in a position where there's an opportunity to advance."

Charles shook his head with doubt, and Mr. Macy's response the following day was just as disappointing.

Dalyrimple had arrived at the office just before it was about to close.

"Mr. Macy, I'd like to speak to you."

"Why—yes." The humorless smile appeared. The voice carried a hint of resentment.

"I want to talk to you about getting a raise."

Mr. Macy nodded.

"Well," he said with uncertainty, "I'm not sure exactly what you're up to. I'll talk to Mr. Hanson."

He understood perfectly what Dalyrimple was up to, and Dalyrimple was aware that he understood.

"I'm in the stockroom—and, sir, while I'm here I'd like to ask you how much longer I'll have to stay there."

"Why—I'm not entirely certain. Naturally, it takes some time to learn the inventory."

"You told me it would take two months when I started."

"Yes. Well, I'll speak to Mr. Hanson."

Dalyrimple hesitated, uncertain what to do.

"Thank you, sir."

Two days later, he showed up at the office again with the results of a count that Mr. Hesse, the bookkeeper, had requested. Mr. Hesse was busy, so Dalyrimple waited and started casually flipping through a ledger that was sitting on the stenographer's desk.

Half unconsciously, he flipped to the next page—he spotted his name—it was a payroll list:

Dalyrimple

Demming

Donahoe

Everett

His eyes stopped—

Everett..........................$60

So Tom Everett, Macy's weak-chinned nephew, had started at sixty dollars a week—and within three weeks he had moved out of the packing room and into the office.

So that was the reality! He would have to sit there and watch as one man after another was promoted above him: sons, cousins, friends' children, regardless of their actual abilities, while he remained stuck as a mere pawn, with "traveling sales work" dangled in front of him as false hope—dismissed with the standard response: "I'll consider it; I'll look into the matter." By age forty, he might end up as a bookkeeper like old Hesse, weary and indifferent Hesse with his monotonous daily grind and the dreary backdrop of boarding-house small talk.

This was a moment when a genius should have placed into his hand the book meant for disillusioned young men. But that book has never been written.

A powerful wave of protest building into rebellion rose within him. Half-remembered ideas, chaotically understood and absorbed, flooded his thoughts. Move forward—that was life's fundamental rule—and that was everything. The method didn't matter—but to become like Hesse or Charley Moore.

"I won't!" he shouted.

The bookkeeper and the stenographers glanced up with surprise.

"What?"

For a moment Dalyrimple stared—then walked up to the desk.

"Here's that data," he said curtly. "I can't wait any longer."

Mr. Hesse's face showed surprise.

It didn't matter what he did—he just needed to escape this endless cycle. In a dreamlike state, he stepped out of the elevator into the stockroom, walked to an empty aisle, sat down on a box, and buried his face in his hands.

His mind was racing with the shocking realization that he had just discovered something completely obvious on his own.

"I have to escape from this," he said out loud and then said again, "I have to get out"—and he wasn't just talking about leaving Macy's wholesale house.

When he left at five-thirty, rain was coming down hard, but he headed in the opposite direction from his boarding house, feeling a strange sense of excitement and renewal in the first cool dampness that seeped wetly through his worn suit. He longed for a world that felt like walking through rain, even if he couldn't see very far ahead, but destiny had placed him in the world of Mr. Macy's stuffy storage rooms and hallways. At first, just an overwhelming desire for change drove him forward, then rough ideas started taking shape in his mind.

"I'll head east to a major city where I can meet people—important people—who will help me find meaningful work. Dear God, there has to be something out there for me."

With disturbing clarity, he realized that his ability to connect with people was restricted. If anywhere, it should have been here in his hometown where he ought to be recognized, where he was indeed recognized—celebrated—before the waters of forgetfulness had washed over him.

You had to cut corners, that was all. Pull—connections—wealthy marriages——

For several miles, this repeated thought consumed his attention until he noticed that the rain had grown heavier and denser in the thick gray twilight, and the houses were becoming fewer. The area of complete city blocks gave way to large houses, then to scattered small ones, and finally vast stretches of foggy countryside spread out on either side. Walking became difficult here. The sidewalk had disappeared, replaced by a dirt road marked with rushing brown streams that splashed and squelched around his shoes.

Cutting corners—the words started to break down, creating strange phrases—small glowing fragments of their original selves. They came together as sentences, each one sounding oddly familiar.

Taking shortcuts meant abandoning the childhood beliefs that success came from being faithful to one's responsibilities, that wrongdoing would inevitably be punished or goodness would inevitably be rewarded—that honest poverty brought more happiness than corrupt wealth.

It meant being tough.

This phrase resonated with him and he kept repeating it again and again. It was somehow connected to Mr. Macy and Charley Moore—their attitudes and their respective approaches.

He stopped and checked his clothing. He was soaked completely through. He glanced around and, choosing a spot along the fence where a tree provided cover, settled himself there.

In my naive years—he thought—they told me that evil was a kind of dirty stain, just as clear-cut as a grimy collar, but it appears to me that evil is simply a form of bad fortune, or genetics-and-circumstances, or "getting caught." It lurks in the wavering of fools like Charley Moore just as surely as it does in the narrow-mindedness of Macy, and if it ever becomes much more concrete it turns into nothing more than a random tag to slap on the disagreeable aspects of other people's lives.

In fact—he concluded—it's not worth worrying about what's evil and what isn't. Good and evil don't mean anything to me as standards—and they can be a terrible obstacle when I want something. When I want something badly enough, common sense tells me to go and take it— and not get caught.

And then suddenly Dalyrimple realized what he needed first. He needed fifteen dollars to pay his overdue board bill.

With intense fury, he leaped down from the fence, tore off his coat, and used his knife to cut a square piece roughly five inches across from the black fabric lining. He punched two holes near the edge and then secured it over his face, tugging his hat down to keep it in position. The makeshift mask fluttered awkwardly before becoming wet and sticking to his forehead and cheeks.

Now... The twilight had blended into a dripping darkness... black as tar. He started walking quickly back toward town, not bothering to take off the mask but peering at the road with difficulty through the rough eye-holes. He wasn't aware of feeling nervous... the only strain came from wanting to get the thing done as quickly as possible.

He reached the first sidewalk and kept walking until he spotted a hedge far from any streetlight, then ducked behind it. Within a minute he heard multiple sets of footsteps approaching—he waited—it was a woman and he held his breath until she walked past . . . and then a man, a worker. The next person to come by, he sensed, would be exactly what he was looking for . . . the worker's footsteps faded far up the rain-soaked street . . . other footsteps grew closer and suddenly became much louder.

Dalyrimple steadied himself.

"Put up your hands!"

The man came to a halt, let out a ridiculous little grunt, and threw his chubby arms up toward the sky.

Dalyrimple searched through the waistcoat.

"Listen here, you little runt," he said, placing his hand meaningfully on his hip pocket, "you better run, and stomp your feet—make it loud! If I hear you stop running, I'll send a bullet your way!"

Then he stood there bursting into sudden, uncontrollable laughter as the sound of frightened footsteps hurried away into the darkness.

After a moment he shoved the roll of cash into his pocket, pulled off his mask, and ran quickly across the street before disappearing down an alley.

Chapter 4

Yet, no matter how Dalyrimple rationalized his choice intellectually, he experienced many difficult moments in the weeks right after making his decision. The enormous weight of emotional attachment and the ambitions passed down to him kept clashing with his mindset. He felt morally isolated.

The afternoon following his first adventure, he had lunch at a small restaurant with Charley Moore and, observing him unfold the newspaper, anticipated some comment about yesterday's robbery. However, either the robbery wasn't reported or Charley showed no interest. He turned without enthusiasm to the sports section, read Doctor Crane's collection of stale platitudes, absorbed an editorial about ambition with his mouth hanging slightly open, and then jumped ahead to Mutt and Jeff.

Poor Charley—with his subtle hint of wickedness and his inability to concentrate, mindlessly playing a dull game of solitaire with discarded trouble.

Yet Charley belonged on the other side of the fence. He could be stirred to passionate outrage and righteous condemnation; he would cry over a stage heroine's lost innocence, and he could become noble and scornful at the thought of disgrace.

On my side, Dalyrimple thought, there aren't any safe havens; a man who's a powerful criminal goes after the weaker criminals too, so it's all guerrilla warfare over here.

What will all of this do to me? he wondered with a lingering exhaustion. Will it drain the vibrancy from life along with my honor? Will it destroy my courage and cloud my thinking?—strip away my spirit entirely—does it lead to emptiness in the end, regret, defeat?

With a powerful wave of rage, he would hurl his thoughts against the obstacle—and remain there with the gleaming blade of his arrogance. Other people who violated the principles of fairness and compassion deceived everyone around them. He, at least, would not deceive himself. He had become more than Byronic at this point: not the spiritual revolutionary, Don Juan; not the philosophical revolutionary, Faust; but a fresh psychological revolutionary of his own era—challenging the emotional preconceived structures of his own consciousness——

Happiness was what he desired—a gradually increasing series of satisfactions for his ordinary desires—and he firmly believed that the components, if not the motivation for happiness, could be purchased with money.

Chapter 5

The night arrived that pulled him out for his second adventure, and as he walked through the dark street he sensed within himself a strong similarity to a cat—a particular flexible, graceful agility. His muscles moved smoothly and elegantly beneath his lean, fit body—he felt a ridiculous urge to leap down the street, to run weaving between trees, to perform cartwheels across soft grass.

The air wasn't sharp, but it carried a subtle hint of tartness that felt inspiring rather than cold.

"The moon has set—I haven't heard the clock strike!"

He laughed with joy at the line that an early memory had given a quiet, breathtaking beauty.

He walked past one man and then encountered another person a quarter mile later.

He was on Philmore Street now and it was very dark. He was grateful to the city council for not installing new streetlights as a recent budget had suggested. There was the red-brick Sterner house that marked the start of the avenue; there was the Jordon house, the Eisenhauers', the Dents', the Markhams', the Frasers'; the Hawkins', where he had been a guest; the Willoughbys', the Everetts', colonial and elaborate; the small cottage where the Watts spinsters lived between the grand facades of the Macys' and the Krupstadts'; the Craigs—

Ah... there! He stopped, trembling intensely—far down the street was a dark figure, a man walking, perhaps a police officer. After what felt like an endless moment, he discovered himself trailing the unclear, jagged shadow of a streetlight across a yard, moving hunched over very low. Then he stood rigid, breathless and not needing air, in the shadow of his limestone target.

He listened endlessly—a mile away a cat howled, and a hundred yards off another picked up the cry in a demonic snarl, making his heart sink and lurch as it cushioned the shock for his mind. Other sounds reached him; the faintest trace of a song in the distance; harsh, chattering laughter from a back porch across the alley; and crickets, crickets chirping in the patched, patterned, moonlit grass of the yard. Inside the house, there seemed to hang a threatening silence. He was grateful he didn't know who lived there.

His slight trembling transformed into steely determination; the steel then softened and his nerves became as flexible as leather; clenching his hands he was relieved to find them nimble, and pulling out his knife and pliers he began working on the screen.

He felt so confident that no one was watching him that, once he reached the dining room moments later, he leaned out and carefully pulled the screen into place, positioning it so that it wouldn't accidentally fall down or create a major barrier if he needed to make a quick escape.

Then he slipped the open knife into his coat pocket, pulled out his flashlight, and quietly tiptoed around the room.

There was nothing here he could use—the dining room had never been part of his plans for the town was too small to allow him to sell off the silver.

In reality, his plans were extremely vague. He had discovered that with a mind like his—rich in intelligence, intuition, and rapid decision-making—it was better to have only the basic framework of a strategy. The machine-gun incident had shown him this lesson. And he worried that a predetermined approach would create conflicting perspectives during a crisis—and having two viewpoints would lead to hesitation.

He stumbled slightly on a chair, held his breath, listened, went on, found the hall, found the stairs, started up; the seventh stair creaked under his step, the ninth, the fourteenth. He was counting them without thinking. At the third creak he stopped again for more than a minute—and in that minute he felt lonelier than he had ever felt in his life. Between the trenches on patrol, even when by himself, he had carried with him the moral backing of half a billion people; now he stood alone, fighting against that very same moral force—an outlaw. He had never experienced this terror, yet he had never experienced this rush of excitement.

The stairs ended, and a doorway came into view; he entered and heard steady breathing. He moved carefully, taking minimal steps, his body occasionally swaying as he reached across the dresser, slipping into his pockets anything that seemed valuable—though he couldn't have listed what he'd taken just ten seconds later. He searched a chair for pants that might be there, but instead found delicate clothing, women's undergarments. The edges of his lips curved into an automatic smile.

Another room... the same breathing, made more intense by one horrible snort that sent his heart racing around his chest again. Round object—watch; chain; roll of bills; stickpins; two rings—he recalled that he had taken rings from the other dresser. He began to move out and flinched as a dim light flashed before him, directly in front of him. God!—it was the glow from his own wristwatch on his extended arm.

Down the stairs. He jumped over two crumbling steps but landed on another one. He was fine now, almost completely safe; as he approached the bottom he experienced a mild sense of boredom. He arrived at the dining room—looked at the silver—once again chose not to take it.

Back in his room at the boarding house, he looked over the new items he had acquired:

Sixty-five dollars in cash.

A platinum ring featuring three medium-sized diamonds, likely valued at around seven hundred dollars. Diamond prices were on the rise.

A cheap gold-plated ring with the initials O. S. and the date inside—'03—probably a class ring from school. Worth a few dollars. Impossible to sell.

A red fabric case holding a set of dentures.

A silver watch.

A gold chain that costs more than the watch itself.

An empty ring box.

A small ivory Chinese figurine—likely a desk decoration.

A dollar and sixty-two cents in small change.

He placed the money beneath his pillow and tucked the remaining items into the toe of a military boot, cramming a sock on top to conceal them. For the next two hours, his thoughts churned frantically like a powerful motor, darting back and forth through his existence—past experiences and future possibilities, moments of terror and joy. With an unclear, poorly-timed longing to have a wife, he drifted into profound slumber around five-thirty.

Chapter 6

Though the newspaper report about the break-in didn't mention the stolen dentures, they troubled him deeply. The image of someone waking up in the chilly morning and searching desperately for their missing teeth, of eating a mushy breakfast without them, of a peculiar, empty voice with a lisp when calling the police, of exhausting and disheartening trips to the dentist, stirred profound compassionate concern within him.

Attempting to determine whether they belonged to a man or a woman, he carefully removed them from the case and brought them close to his mouth. He moved his own jaw experimentally and took measurements with his fingers, but he couldn't reach a conclusion: they could have belonged to either a woman with a large mouth or a man with a small mouth.

Acting on a sudden impulse, he wrapped them in brown paper he found at the bottom of his military trunk and wrote "false teeth" on the package using awkward pencil lettering. The following evening, he walked down Philmore Street and tossed the package onto the lawn so it would land close to the door. The next day, the newspaper reported that the police had a lead—they knew the burglar was still in town. However, they didn't reveal what that lead was.

Chapter 7

At the end of a month, "Burglar Bill of the Silver District" had become the go-to story nursemaids used to scare children. Five break-ins were blamed on him, but even though Dalyrimple had only carried out three of them, he figured the majority ruled and claimed the nickname for himself. He had been spotted once—"a big, bloated man with the most wicked face you've ever seen." Mrs. Henry Coleman, who woke up at two in the morning with an electric flashlight beam shining in her eyes, couldn't have been expected to identify Bryan Dalyrimple, the same person she had waved flags at during the last Fourth of July celebration and had once described as "not really the reckless type, don't you think?"

When Dalrymple kept his imagination burning intensely, he succeeded in making his own perspective seem noble, celebrating his freedom from minor guilt and regret—but the moment he let his thoughts wander unprotected, terrible unexpected fears and sadness would overwhelm him. For comfort, he would then need to return and think through the entire situation once more. He discovered that overall it was better to stop viewing himself as someone fighting against the system. It was more comforting to consider everyone else as foolish.

His feelings toward Mr. Macy began to shift. He no longer experienced that vague hostility and sense of inadequacy when around him. By the time his fourth month at the store came to an end, he found himself looking at his boss in an almost brotherly way. He held a fuzzy yet confident belief that Mr. Macy's deepest spirit would have supported and endorsed what he was doing. His concerns about the future had disappeared. His plan was to save up several thousand dollars before leaving—heading east, returning to France, or traveling down to South America. During the past two months, he had come close to quitting his job at least six times, but his worry about drawing attention to his newfound wealth held him back. So he continued working, no longer with apathy, but with scornful entertainment.

_____

Chapter 8

Then with remarkable suddenness, something occurred that altered his plans and brought his burglaries to an end.

Mr. Macy called for him one afternoon and with an elaborate display of cheerful secrecy inquired whether he had any plans for that evening. If he was free, would he kindly visit Mr. Alfred J. Fraser at eight o'clock. Dalyrimple's curiosity mixed with apprehension. He wondered whether he should catch the next train and leave town immediately. However, after an hour of thinking it over, he concluded that his worries were groundless, and at eight o'clock he reached the large Fraser residence on Philmore Avenue.

Mr. Fraser was widely considered to be the most powerful political figure in the city. His brother served as Senator Fraser, his son-in-law held the position of Congressman Demming, and his influence, while not exercised in a manner that would make him an undesirable political boss, remained substantial nonetheless.

He had a large, imposing face with deeply recessed eyes and an enormous upper lip, all coming together in a distinctly professional-looking elongated jaw.

During his conversation with Dalyrimple, his facial expression kept beginning to form a smile, reached a state of cheerful optimism, and then retreated back to complete composure.

"How are you, sir?" he said, extending his hand. "Please, have a seat. I imagine you're curious about why I asked you to come. Sit down."

Dalyrimple sat down.

"Mr. Dalyrimple, how old are you?"

"I'm twenty-three."

"You're young. But that doesn't mean you're foolish. Mr. Dalyrimple, what I have to say won't take long. I'm going to make you an offer. To start from the beginning, I've been watching you ever since last Fourth of July when you gave that speech in response to the loving-cup."

Dalyrimple muttered dismissively, but Fraser gestured for him to be quiet.

"It was a speech I'll never forget. It was an intelligent speech, direct and honest, and it reached everyone in that audience. I know this because I've been observing crowds for years." He cleared his throat as though he might elaborate on his understanding of crowds—then went on. "But, Mr. Dalyrimple, I've witnessed too many promising young men fall apart, fail because they lacked consistency, had too many ambitious ideas, and weren't willing enough to put in the work. So I waited. I wanted to see what you would do. I wanted to see if you would get to work, and if you would stick with what you began."

Dalyrimple felt a warm feeling wash over him.

"So," Fraser went on, "when Theron Macy told me you'd begun working at his place, I kept an eye on you, and I tracked your progress through him. During the first month I was worried for a while. He told me you were becoming restless, acting like you were too good for your position, dropping hints about wanting a raise——"

Dalyrimple was startled.

"But he said that afterward you clearly decided to keep quiet and stick with that decision. That's the kind of attitude I admire in a young person! That's what leads to success. And don't think I don't get it. I understand how much more difficult it became for you after all that foolish praise those old women had been showering you with. I know what a struggle it must have been——"

Dalyrimple's face was burning bright red. It felt youthful and surprisingly innocent.

"Dalyrimple, you're intelligent and you have what it takes—and that's exactly what I'm looking for. I'm going to get you into the State Senate."

"The what?"

"The State Senate. We need a young man who's intelligent but reliable and not lazy. And when I mention the State Senate, I'm not stopping there. We're facing a real challenge here, Dalyrimple. We have to bring some young people into politics—you understand how the same old guard has been running on the party ticket year after year."

Dalyrimple licked his lips.

"You'll run me for the State Senate?"

"I'll get you a seat in the State Senate."

Mr. Fraser's face had almost formed a smile, and Dalyrimple, feeling playfully optimistic, found himself mentally encouraging it to continue—but it froze, became rigid, and disappeared. The barn door and his jaw were divided by a line as straight as a nail. Dalyrimple had to remind himself that it was actually a mouth, and he spoke to it.

"But I'm finished," he said. "My fame has died out. People are sick of me."

"Those things," Mr. Fraser replied, "are just mechanical processes. The Linotype machine can bring dead reputations back to life. Just wait until you see the Herald starting next week—assuming you're going to work with us—that is," and his tone became a bit sharper, "assuming you don't have too many of your own ideas about how things should be managed."

"No," said Dalyrimple, looking him directly in the eye. "You'll need to give me plenty of guidance at the beginning."

"Very well. I'll take care of your reputation then. Just keep yourself on the right side of the fence."

Dalyrimple was startled by hearing this phrase repeated—the same words that had been occupying his thoughts so frequently in recent days. Suddenly, the doorbell rang.

"That's Macy now," Fraser noted, getting up. "I'll go let him in. The servants have gone to bed."

He left Dalyrimple there in a daze. The world was suddenly opening up before him—the State Senate, the

United States Senate—so this was what life was really about—taking shortcuts—using common sense, that was the key. No more foolish chances now unless absolutely necessary—but it was being tough that mattered—Never let guilt or self-blame cost him a night's sleep—let his life be a weapon of bravery—there was no price to pay—all that was nonsense—complete nonsense.

He jumped up with clenched fists in a kind of triumph.

"Well, Bryan," said Mr. Macy as he stepped through the curtains.

The two older men gave him their half-smiles.

"Well Bryan," Mr. Macy said again.

Dalyrimple smiled as well.

"How are you doing, Mr. Macy?"

He wondered if some kind of telepathic connection between them had made this newfound understanding possible—some unseen awareness. . . .

Mr. Macy extended his hand.

"I'm happy that we're going to be working together on this plan—I've been supporting you from the beginning—particularly recently. I'm pleased that we're going to be on the same team."

"I want to thank you, sir," Dalrymple said simply. He felt an odd moisture forming behind his eyes.

The Four Fists

Chapter 1

At the present time, no one I know has the slightest desire to hit Samuel Meredith; perhaps this is because a man over fifty is likely to be rather severely injured by the impact of an aggressive fist, but I personally believe that all his hitable qualities have completely disappeared. However, it is certain that at various points in his life, hitable qualities were present in his face, just as surely as kissable qualities have ever existed in a girl's lips.

I'm certain everyone has encountered someone like that—been casually introduced to him, perhaps even befriended him, yet sensed he was the type who stirred up intense hatred. Some people showed this through the automatic clenching of their fists, while others expressed it through grumbling about "taking a swing" and "landing a quick punch in the eye." In Samuel Meredith's facial features, this characteristic was so pronounced that it shaped his whole existence.

What was it? Certainly not his appearance, since he had been good-looking from his early years: he had a broad forehead and gray eyes that were honest and warm. Yet I've heard him tell a roomful of reporters who were fishing for a "success" story that he would be embarrassed to tell them the real truth because they wouldn't believe it, that it wasn't just one story but four different ones, and that the public wouldn't want to read about a man who had been beaten into fame.

It all began at Phillips Andover Academy when he was fourteen years old. He had been raised on a steady diet of caviar and luxury in half the capital cities of Europe, and it was simply fortunate that his mother suffered a nervous breakdown and had to hand over his education to less indulgent, more objective guardians.

At Andover, Samuel was assigned a roommate named Gilly Hood. Gilly was thirteen years old, small for his age, and somewhat of a favorite among the school community. From the September day when Mr. Meredith's personal servant unpacked Samuel's clothes into the finest dresser and asked, before leaving, "if there was anything else, Master Samuel?" Gilly complained that the faculty had betrayed him. He felt like an angry frog whose bowl had been invaded by goldfish.

"Good grief!" he grumbled to his understanding friends, "he's such a conceited snob. He asked, 'Are the people here gentlemen?' and I replied, 'No, they're just boys,' and he said age wasn't important, and I responded, 'Who said it was?' Let him try to mess with me, that old fool!"

For three weeks, Gilly quietly put up with young Samuel's remarks about his friends' clothing and behavior, tolerated the French phrases sprinkled throughout their conversations, and suffered through countless petty, almost feminine cruelties that reveal what an anxious mother can inflict on her son when she hovers too closely—then chaos erupted in the aquarium.

Samuel was away. A group of people had come together to listen to Gilly angrily complain about his roommate's recent wrongdoings.

"He said, 'Oh, I don't like the windows open at night,' he said, 'except only a little bit,'" Gilly complained.

"Don't let him boss you around."

"Boss me around? You can bet he won't. I open those windows, I suppose, but the stubborn fool won't take turns closing them in the morning."

"Make him, Gilly, why don't you?"

"I'm going to." Gilly nodded his head with fierce determination. "Don't you worry. He doesn't need to think I'm just some ordinary butler."

"Let's see you make him."

At this point the damn fool walked in and flashed one of his annoying smiles at the crowd. Two boys said, "Hey, Meredith"; the others shot him a cold look and continued talking to Gilly. But Samuel seemed unsatisfied.

"Could you please not sit on my bed?" he asked politely to two of Gilly's friends who were sitting there quite comfortably.

"Huh?"

"My bed. Can't you understand English?"

This was adding insult to injury. There were several comments about the bed's unsanitary condition and the clear signs of insects or other pests living in it.

"What's wrong with your old bed?" Gilly asked aggressively.

"The bed's fine, but——"

Gilly cut off this sentence by standing up and walking over to Samuel. He stopped just a few inches away and stared at him intensely.

"You and your crazy old bed," he began. "You and your crazy——"

"Go for it, Gilly," someone whispered.

"Show the darn fool——"

Samuel returned the look with calm composure.

"Well," he said finally, "it's my bed——"

He didn't get any further because Gilly drew back and punched him squarely in the nose.

"Yes! Gilly!"

"Show the big bully!"

"Just let him touch you—he'll see!"

The group surrounded them, and for the first time in his life Samuel understood the overwhelming disadvantage of being intensely hated. He looked around desperately at the scowling, furiously angry faces. He stood a full head taller than his roommate, so if he fought back he would be labeled a bully and face half a dozen additional fights within five minutes; however, if he didn't fight back he would be considered a coward. For a moment he remained there confronting Gilly's furious eyes, and then, with a sudden strangled noise, he pushed his way through the circle and fled from the room.

The following month contained the thirty most miserable days of his entire life. During every moment he was awake, his classmates attacked him with cruel words; his behaviors and quirks became targets for unbearable jokes and, naturally, the emotional sensitivity that comes with being a teenager made everything worse. He believed he was destined to be an outcast; that being unpopular at school would haunt him for the rest of his life. When he went home for Christmas break, he felt so hopeless that his father took him to see a doctor who specialized in nervous conditions. When he came back to Andover, he planned to arrive late so he would be the only one on the bus during the trip from the train station to school.

Of course, once he had learned to keep quiet, everyone quickly forgot all about him. The following autumn, having realized that being considerate of others was the wise approach, he took full advantage of the fresh beginning that

94

came with how quickly boys forget things. By the start of his senior year, Samuel Meredith had become one of the most popular boys in his class—and no one supported him more than his first friend and loyal companion, Gilly Hood.

Chapter 2

Samuel became the type of college student who, in the early 1890s, drove horse-drawn carriages, coaches, and large passenger vehicles between Princeton and Yale and New York City to demonstrate their appreciation for the social significance of football games. He was deeply passionate about proper etiquette—the way he selected his gloves, knotted his ties, and gripped the reins was copied by easily influenced first-year students. Those outside his social circle viewed him as somewhat snobbish, but since his group was the dominant one, this never bothered him. He played football during the fall season, consumed whiskey cocktails throughout the winter months, and participated in rowing during the spring. Samuel looked down upon anyone who was simply an athlete without being a gentleman or merely a gentleman without being an athlete.

He lived in New York and frequently invited several of his friends home for the weekend. These were the times of horse-drawn streetcars, and when the car was crowded, it was naturally expected that anyone from Samuel's social circle would stand up and offer his seat to a lady who was standing, accompanied by a polite bow. One evening during Samuel's third year of college, he got on a streetcar with two of his close friends. There were three empty seats available. When Samuel took his seat, he noticed a weary-looking working man sitting beside him who had an unpleasant smell of garlic, leaned slightly against Samuel, and stretched out somewhat as exhausted men do, occupying far too much space.

The car had traveled several blocks when it came to a stop for four young women, and naturally, the three sophisticated gentlemen immediately jumped up and offered their seats with proper etiquette. Unfortunately, the working man, being unfamiliar with the social rules of well-dressed society, didn't follow their lead, leaving one young woman standing awkwardly. Fourteen eyes stared at him with disapproval; seven mouths showed slight disgust; but the target of their contempt gazed steadily ahead, completely unaware of his shameful behavior. Samuel was the most deeply disturbed by this. He felt embarrassed that any man would act this way. He spoke out loud.

"There's a lady standing," he said sternly.

That should have been more than sufficient, but the target of ridicule simply stared up with a vacant expression. The girl who was standing giggled nervously and shared anxious looks with her friends. However, Samuel had become agitated.

"There's a lady standing," he said again, his voice rough and grating. The man appeared to understand.

"I pay my fare," he said quietly.

Samuel's face flushed red and his hands clenched into fists, but the conductor was watching them, so when his friends gave him a warning nod, he sank back into moody silence.

They arrived at their destination and got out of the car, but the worker did too, following behind them while swinging his small bucket. Seeing his opportunity, Samuel no longer fought against his upper-class tendencies. He turned around and, displaying a complete, melodramatic sneer, made a loud comment about whether lower creatures should be allowed to travel alongside human beings.

In half a second, the worker had dropped his bucket and thrown a punch at him. Caught off guard, Samuel took the hit squarely on the jaw and fell flat into the cobblestone gutter.

"Don't laugh at me!" shouted his attacker. "I've been working all day. I'm exhausted!"

As he spoke, the sudden anger faded from his eyes and the mask of exhaustion settled over his face once more. He turned around and picked up his bucket. Samuel's friends quickly stepped toward him.

"Wait!" Samuel had gotten up slowly and was gesturing for them to stop. At some point, somewhere, he had been hit like that before. Then he recalled—Gilly Hood. In the quiet, as he brushed himself off, the entire scene in the room at Andover appeared before him—and he understood instinctively that he had been mistaken again. This man's power, his peace, came from protecting his family. He needed his seat on the streetcar more than any young woman did.

"It's all right," Samuel said roughly. "Don't touch him. I've been a damn fool."

Of course it took more than an hour, or a week, for Samuel to reorganize his thoughts about the crucial importance of proper etiquette. Initially he simply acknowledged that his error had left him helpless—just as it had rendered him powerless against Gilly—but gradually his misjudgment about the laborer transformed his whole perspective. Snobbery is, ultimately, nothing more than good manners turned tyrannical; therefore Samuel's principles remained intact but the compulsion to force them on others had disappeared in a particular gutter. Before that year ended his classmates had somehow ceased calling him a snob.

Chapter 3

After a few years, Samuel's university decided it had basked long enough in the reflected glory of his stylish neckties, so they delivered a formal declaration to him in Latin, charged him ten dollars for the diploma that certified he was thoroughly educated, and sent him out into the chaos of the real world with plenty of self-confidence, a handful of friends, and the typical collection of harmless bad habits.

His family had already begun their return to working-class status due to a sudden crash in the sugar market, and they had essentially loosened their financial belt, so to speak, by the time Samuel started working. His mind was that perfect blank slate that a university education sometimes creates, but he possessed both drive and connections, so he applied his former skills as an elusive half-back to navigate through Wall Street crowds while working as a messenger for a bank.

His entertainment was—women. There were about six of them: two or three young women making their social debut, an actress (though not a particularly successful one), a divorced woman, and one romantic little dark-haired woman who was married and lived in a small house in Jersey City.

They had met on a ferry. Samuel was traveling from New York for work (he had been employed for several years by then) and he helped her search for a package she had lost in the crowd.

"Do you come here often?" he asked casually.

"Just to shop," she said shyly. She had large brown eyes and a pitiful little mouth. "I've only been married three months, and we've discovered it's more affordable to live over here."

"Does he—does your husband like you being alone like this?"

She laughed, a cheerful young laugh.

"Oh no, definitely not. We were supposed to meet for dinner, but I must have gotten the location wrong. He's going to be really worried."

"Well," Samuel said with disapproval, "he should be. If you don't mind, I'll walk you home."

She gratefully accepted his offer, and they rode the cable car together. As they walked up the path to her small house, they noticed a light was on; her husband had gotten there before she did.

"He's extremely jealous," she said with an apologetic laugh.

"Alright," Samuel replied, somewhat coldly. "I should probably leave you here."

She thanked him and, waving goodnight, he left her.

That would have been the end of it if they hadn't run into each other on Fifth Avenue one morning a week later. She jumped with surprise and her cheeks turned red, and she seemed so happy to see him that they talked like old friends. She was heading to her dressmaker's, planning to eat lunch by herself at Taine's, spend the whole afternoon shopping, and then meet her husband at the ferry at five o'clock. Samuel told her that her husband was a very fortunate man. Her face flushed red again and she hurried away.

Samuel whistled during his entire walk back to the office, but around noon he started seeing that pitiful, pleading little mouth everywhere—along with those brown eyes. He grew restless whenever he glanced at the clock; he pictured the restaurant downstairs where he usually ate lunch and its serious masculine chatter, but against that image emerged another scene: a small table at Taine's with those brown eyes and that mouth just a few feet away. A few minutes before twelve-thirty he grabbed his hat and hurried toward the cable car.

She was completely shocked to see him.

"Why—hello," she said. Samuel could see that she was just pleasantly startled.

"I thought we could have lunch together. It's so boring eating with a bunch of men."

She hesitated.

"Well, I don't see any harm in it. How could there be!"

She realized that her husband should have had lunch with her, but he was usually so rushed at midday. She told Samuel everything about him: he was a bit shorter than Samuel, but oh, much more handsome. He worked as a bookkeeper and wasn't earning much money, but they were very happy and expected to become wealthy within three or four years.

Samuel's estranged wife had been in a quarrelsome mood for three or four weeks, and by contrast, he found heightened pleasure in this encounter; she was so refreshing, sincere, and subtly adventurous. Her name was Marjorie.

They arranged to meet again; in fact, for an entire month they had lunch together two or three times each week. When she was certain that her husband would be working late, Samuel would take her across to New Jersey on the ferry, always leaving her at the small front porch after she had entered and turned on the gas light, using the reassurance of his masculine presence waiting outside. This became a ritual—and it irritated him. Whenever the warm light spilled out through the front windows, that served as his signal to leave; yet he never proposed coming inside and Marjorie never invited him in.

Then, when Samuel and Marjorie had reached a point where they would sometimes gently touch each other's arms, simply to show they were very close friends, Marjorie and her husband had one of those extremely sensitive, highly critical arguments that couples only have when they care deeply about each other. It began with a cold lamb chop or a gas leak—and one day Samuel found her at Taine's, with dark circles under her brown eyes and a frightening sulk.

By this point, Samuel believed he was falling in love with Marjorie, so he made the most of their argument. He became her closest confidant, gently holding her hand and leaning in close to her brown curls as she tearfully shared what her husband had said to her that morning. He stepped beyond the role of just a friend when he escorted her to the ferry in a horse-drawn cab.

"Marjorie," he said softly as he left her on the porch as he always did, "if you ever need me, remember that I'm always here waiting, always waiting."

She nodded seriously and placed both her hands in his. "I know," she said. "I know you're my friend, my best friend."

Then she rushed into the house and he stood there watching until the lights came on.

For the following week, Samuel found himself in a state of anxious confusion. A stubborn voice of reason kept reminding him that fundamentally, he and Marjorie shared very little common ground, but in situations like these, emotions tend to cloud judgment so thoroughly that it becomes nearly impossible to see things clearly. Every fantasy and longing convinced him that he was in love with Marjorie, that he needed her, that he simply had to make her his.

The argument escalated. Marjorie's husband started staying in New York until late at night, returned home several times unpleasantly intoxicated, and made her life generally miserable. They probably had too much pride to discuss it openly—since Marjorie's husband was, fundamentally, a fairly good man—so the situation continued drifting from one misunderstanding to the next. Marjorie increasingly turned to Samuel; when a woman can receive masculine understanding, it proves far more comforting to her than confiding in another woman. However, Marjorie didn't recognize how dependent she had become on him, how integral he had become to her small world.

One night, instead of walking away when Marjorie went inside and turned on the gas light, Samuel followed her in, and they sat together on the couch in the small living room. He felt incredibly happy. He admired their home and believed that any man who would neglect such a treasure out of stubborn pride was a fool who didn't deserve his wife. But when he kissed Marjorie for the first time, she cried quietly and asked him to leave. He went home filled with desperate excitement, completely determined to nurture this spark of romance, regardless of how intense the passion became or who might get hurt. At that moment, he believed his thoughts were selflessly focused on her; looking back later, he realized that she had meant no more to him than a blank movie screen—it was simply Samuel being blind and driven by desire.

The next day at Taine's, when they met for lunch, Samuel abandoned all pretense and openly expressed his love for her. He had no specific plans or clear intentions, except to kiss her lips once more, to hold her close and feel how small and vulnerable and endearing she was. He walked her home, and this time they kissed until both their hearts were racing—words and phrases came to his lips.

And then suddenly there were footsteps on the porch—a hand tried the front door. Marjorie turned completely pale.

"Wait!" she whispered to Samuel, her voice filled with fear, but he was so irritated by the interruption that he stormed to the front door and flung it open.

Everyone has witnessed such scenes on stage—seen them so frequently that when they actually occur in real life, people behave very much like actors. Samuel felt he was performing a role, and the words came quite naturally: he declared that everyone had the right to live their own lives and stared at Marjorie's husband threateningly, as if challenging him to question it. Marjorie's husband spoke about the sanctity of the home, forgetting that it hadn't felt very sacred to him recently; Samuel continued with his speech about "the right to happiness"; Marjorie's husband brought up firearms and the divorce court. Then suddenly he paused and examined both of them—Marjorie collapsed pitifully on the sofa, Samuel lecturing the furniture while striking a deliberately heroic pose.

"Go upstairs, Marjorie," he said, in a different tone.

"Stay where you are!" Samuel shot back immediately.

Marjorie stood up, hesitated, and sat back down, then rose once more and walked uncertainly toward the stairs.

"Come outside," her husband said to Samuel. "I need to talk to you."

Samuel looked at Marjorie, trying to read some kind of message in her eyes; then he pressed his lips together and left the room.

There was a bright moon, and when Marjorie's husband came down the steps, Samuel could clearly see that he was in pain—but he felt no sympathy for him.

They stood facing each other, separated by just a few feet, and the husband cleared his throat as if it had become slightly rough.

"That's my wife," he said quietly, and then a fierce rage erupted within him. "Damn you!" he shouted—and struck Samuel in the face with all his force.

In that instant, as Samuel collapsed to the ground, it struck him that he had been struck like this twice before, and at the same time the situation transformed like a dream—he suddenly felt wide awake. Without thinking, he jumped to his feet and took a fighting stance. The other man stood waiting, fists raised, a yard away, but Samuel realized that even though he had the physical advantage of several inches in height and many pounds in weight, he wouldn't strike him. The circumstances had completely and miraculously shifted—just moments earlier Samuel had felt like a hero; now he felt like the villain, the intruder, while Marjorie's husband, outlined against the glow from the small house, appeared as the timeless heroic figure, the protector of his home.

There was a pause, and then Samuel quickly turned away and walked down the path for the final time.

Chapter 4

Naturally, following the third blow, Samuel spent several weeks engaged in careful self-examination. The blow he had received years earlier at Andover had struck at his personal disagreeableness; the workman during his college years had shaken the snobbery from his character, and Marjorie's husband had delivered a harsh shock to his greedy self-centeredness. This experience removed women from his thoughts entirely until a year later, when he encountered his future wife; the only type of woman who seemed worthwhile was one who could be shielded as Marjorie's husband had shielded her. Samuel could not picture his grass-widow, Mrs. De Ferriac, provoking any particularly justified blows on her own behalf.

By his early thirties, he had established himself quite well. He worked alongside old Peter Carhart, who was a prominent national figure during that era. Carhart possessed the build of a rough-hewn Hercules statue, and his reputation was equally impressive—wealth accumulated purely for the satisfaction of it, without resorting to underhanded tactics or questionable dealings. He had maintained a strong friendship with Samuel's father, yet he observed the son for six years before bringing him into his own firm. Only heaven could account for the vast number of enterprises he controlled during that period—mining operations, railway systems, financial institutions, entire municipalities. Samuel worked closely with him, understanding his preferences and aversions, his biases, his vulnerabilities, and his numerous strengths.

One day Carhart called for Samuel and, after closing the door to his private office, offered him a chair and a cigar.

"Everything okay, Samuel?" he asked.

"Why, yes."

"I've been worried that you're becoming a bit stagnant."

"Stale?" Samuel was confused.

"You haven't done any work outside the office for almost ten years?"

"But I've had vacations, in the Adiron———"

Carhart dismissed this with a wave of his hand.

"I mean outside of work. Watching things happen that we've always been controlling from behind the scenes here."

"No," Samuel admitted; "I haven't."

"So," he said suddenly, "I'm going to give you an assignment outside the office that will take about a month."

Samuel didn't argue. He actually liked the idea and decided that whatever it involved, he would carry it out exactly as Carhart wanted. This was his employer's favorite pastime, and the men working for him followed direct orders without question, just like junior military officers.

"You'll go to San Antonio and see Hamil," Carhart went on. "He's got a job that needs doing and he wants someone to take charge of it."

Hamil managed the Carhart business interests throughout the Southwest, a man who had developed his career under his employer's influence, and although he and Samuel had never met face to face, they had exchanged extensive official correspondence.

"When do I leave?"

"You should leave tomorrow," Carhart replied, looking at the calendar. "That's May 1st. I'll be waiting for your report here on June 1st."

The next morning Samuel departed for Chicago, and two days afterward he found himself sitting across from Hamil at a table in the Merchants' Trust office in San Antonio. Understanding the situation didn't require much time. This was a major oil transaction involving the purchase of seventeen massive neighboring ranches. The acquisition had to be completed within one week, and it was essentially a financial squeeze play. Certain forces had been put into motion that placed the seventeen property owners in an impossible position, and Samuel's role was simply to "manage" the operation from a small town near Pueblo. With the right combination of diplomacy and competence, the right person could execute the plan smoothly without creating any conflict, since it was basically a matter of taking control and maintaining a steady grip. Hamil, with a shrewdness that had proven extremely valuable to his boss on many occasions, had created a scenario that would yield far greater net profits than any transaction conducted through normal market channels. Samuel shook hands with Hamil, made arrangements to return in two weeks, and departed for San Felipe, New Mexico.

It crossed his mind, naturally, that Carhart was testing him. Hamil's assessment of how he managed this situation could influence something significant for his future, but even without that possibility he would have given his all to see it through. A decade in New York hadn't turned him into a sentimentalist and he was completely used to completing everything he started—and then some.

Everything started smoothly. There wasn't any excitement, but each of the seventeen ranchers involved understood Samuel's business dealings, recognized what resources he had backing him, and realized they had about as much chance of resisting as flies stuck to a window. Some had accepted their fate—others were furious about it, but they had discussed the situation, consulted with attorneys and couldn't find any way out. Five of the ranches contained oil, while the remaining twelve were part of the gamble, though equally essential to Hamil's plan regardless.

Samuel quickly realized that the true leader was an early settler named McIntyre, a man around fifty years old, with gray hair, a clean-shaven face, skin bronzed from forty New Mexico summers, and those clear, steady eyes that the Texas and New Mexico climate tends to produce. His ranch hadn't yet shown signs of oil, but it was located within the pool, and if anyone despised the thought of losing his land, it was McIntyre. Everyone had initially looked to him to prevent the major disaster, and he had searched throughout the entire territory for legal methods to accomplish this, but he had been unsuccessful, and he was aware of his failure. He deliberately avoided Samuel, but Samuel was certain that when the time came for signing, McIntyre would show up.

It arrived—a scorching May day, with heat waves shimmering off the dried earth as far as the eye could see, and as Samuel sat sweating in his small makeshift office—a few chairs, a bench, and a wooden table—he felt relieved that the whole ordeal was nearly finished. He desperately wanted to return East and reunite with his wife and children for a week at the beach.

The meeting was scheduled for four o'clock, so he was quite surprised when the door opened at three-thirty and McIntyre walked in. Samuel couldn't help but admire the man's demeanor and feel somewhat sympathetic toward him. McIntyre appeared deeply connected to the prairie lands, and Samuel experienced that brief spark of jealousy that urban dwellers often feel toward those who live in wide-open spaces.

"Good afternoon," McIntyre said, standing in the open doorway with his feet spread apart and his hands resting on his hips.

"Hello, Mr. McIntyre." Samuel stood up, but skipped the formal gesture of extending his hand. He figured the rancher probably despised him completely, and he couldn't really fault him for it. McIntyre walked in and settled into his seat without hurrying.

"You got us," he said suddenly.

This didn't seem to need any response.

"When I found out Carhart was behind this," he went on, "I gave up."

"Mr. Carhart is——" Samuel started to say, but McIntyre gestured for him to be quiet.

"Don't talk about the dirty sneak-thief!"

"Mr. McIntyre," Samuel said briskly, "if we're going to spend this half-hour on that kind of conversation——"

"Oh, shut up, young man," McIntyre interrupted, "you can't criticize a man who would do something like this."

Samuel made no answer.

"It's just plain theft. There are simply people like him who are too powerful to deal with."

"You're being paid generously," Samuel said.

"Be quiet!" McIntyre shouted abruptly. "I need to be the one speaking right now." He moved toward the door and gazed out over the countryside, the bright, humid grassland that started nearly at his doorstep and stretched all the way to the blue-gray peaks of the far-off mountains. When he faced back around, his lips were shaking.

"Do you guys love Wall Street?" he said in a rough voice, "or wherever you carry out your underhanded plotting——" He stopped speaking. "I guess you do. No person sinks so low that they don't somehow love the place where they've worked, where they've poured out the best they had to give."

Samuel watched him uncomfortably. McIntyre wiped his forehead with a large blue handkerchief and went on:

"I figure this corrupt old devil needed another million. I think we're just some of the poor people he's destroyed to buy a couple more carriages or something." He gestured toward the door. "I built a house out there when I was seventeen, with these two hands. I married a woman there at twenty-one, added two wings, and started out with four scrawny steers. For forty summers I've watched the sun rise

109

over those mountains and set red as blood in the evening, before the heat drifted away and the stars appeared. I was happy in that house. My son was born there and he died there, late one spring, in the hottest part of an afternoon like this. Then my wife and I lived there alone like we had before, and tried to make it feel like a home, not a real home but close to it—because the boy always seemed nearby somehow, and we expected many nights to see him running up the path for supper." His voice was trembling so much he could barely speak and he turned again toward the door, his gray eyes narrowed.

"That's my land out there," he said, extending his arm, "my land, by God—It's all I have in the world—and all I ever wanted." He wiped his sleeve across his face, and his tone shifted as he turned slowly and faced Samuel. "But I suppose it has to go when they want it—it has to go."

Samuel had to speak. He felt that in another minute he would completely lose control. So he started talking, keeping his voice as steady as he could—using the kind of tone he reserved for unpleasant tasks.

"It's business, Mr. McIntyre," he said. "It's within the law. Maybe we couldn't have bought out two or three of you at any price, but most of you did have a price. Progress requires certain things———"

Never before had he felt so completely out of his depth, and when he heard the sound of hoofbeats just a few hundred yards in the distance, he experienced tremendous relief.

But when he spoke those words, the sorrow in McIntyre's eyes transformed into rage.

"You and your dirty gang of crooks!" he cried. "Not one of you has genuine love for anything on this earth! You're nothing but a bunch of money-obsessed pigs!"

Samuel stood up and McIntyre moved a step closer to him.

"You talk too much, man. You stole our land—take that for Peter Carhart!"

He threw a punch from his shoulder as quick as lightning, and Samuel collapsed in a heap. Through the haze, he heard footsteps in the doorway and realized someone was restraining McIntyre, but it wasn't necessary. The rancher had slumped back into his chair and buried his head in his hands.

Samuel's mind was racing. He understood that the fourth punch had struck him, and an overwhelming surge of feelings screamed that the law which had relentlessly governed his existence was operating once more. In a confused state, he stood up and walked quickly out of the room.

The following ten minutes were probably the most difficult he had ever experienced. People often speak about having the courage of your convictions, but in real life, a person's responsibility to their family can make sticking rigidly to your principles seem like a selfish way of satisfying your own sense of being right. Samuel's thoughts were mainly focused on his family, but he never truly hesitated. That shock had brought him back to reality.

When he returned to the room, many worried faces were waiting for him, but he didn't waste any time explaining.

"Gentlemen," he said, "Mr. McIntyre has been generous enough to persuade me that in this situation you are completely right and the Peter Carhart interests are completely wrong. As far as I'm concerned, you can keep your ranches for the rest of your lives."

He pushed through the shocked crowd, and within thirty minutes he had sent two telegrams that left the telegraph operator completely unable to continue working; one went to Hamil in San Antonio, and the other to Peter Carhart in New York.

Samuel barely slept that night. He understood that for the first time in his business career, he had suffered a complete and devastating failure. Yet something within him—an instinct more powerful than willpower, more profound than any training he'd received—had compelled him to take action that would likely destroy both his ambitions and his happiness. But the deed was done, and it never crossed his mind that he could have chosen a different path.

The next morning, two telegrams were waiting for him. The first one was from Hamil. It contained three words:

"You blamed idiot!"

The second was from New York:

"Deal off come to New York immediately Carhart."

Within a week, events unfolded rapidly. Hamil argued fiercely and passionately defended his plan. He was called to New York and endured a difficult thirty minutes being reprimanded in Peter Carhart's office. He severed ties with the Carhart business interests in July, and by August, Samuel Meredith, at thirty-five years of age, had essentially become Carhart's partner. The fourth blow had accomplished its purpose.

I believe there's a selfish streak in every man that cuts across his character, personality, and general perspective. In some men it stays hidden, and we never realize it exists until they betray us unexpectedly. But Samuel's showed itself when it was active, and seeing it made people furious. He was somewhat fortunate in this regard, because every time his inner demon emerged it encountered such strong opposition that it retreated weakened and defeated. It was this same demon, this same streak that drove him to kick Gilly's friends off the bed, that compelled him to enter Marjorie's house.

If you could run your hand along Samuel Meredith's jaw, you'd feel a bump. He confesses he's never been certain which punch left it there, but he wouldn't give it up for the world. He claims there's no scoundrel like an experienced scoundrel, and that occasionally just before reaching a decision, it helps tremendously to rub his chin. The journalists describe it as a nervous habit, but that's not what it is. It's so he can experience once more the magnificent clarity, the brilliant lucidity of those four punches.

THE END

Thank You For Reading

You've Just Read a Piece of the Greatest Library Ever Rebuilt

Thank you for reading.

This book is one of thousands we're restoring, reimagining, and translating as part of the **Modern Library of Alexandria** — a global movement to preserve and share humanity's most important ideas.

What was once lost to fire and time is now rising again — not just as memory, but as living, breathing knowledge, freely accessible to all.

What You Can Do Next:

*   **Keep Reading.**

    Discover more legendary works — in beautiful print, audiobook, or digital form — at LibraryofAlexandria.com.

*   **Build Your Own Library.**

    Every title is available as a paperback, hardcover, or collectible boxset — at true printing cost. Craft a personal library worthy of display.

*   **Spread the Light.**

    Share this book. Tell others about the movement. Help us translate every timeless work into every language, so no reader is ever left behind.

By finishing this book, you've already taken part in something extraordinary.

Join us at LibraryofAlexandria.com

Together, we're rebuilding the greatest library the world has ever known.

With appreciation,

The Modern Library of Alexandria Team

Visit:
www.libraryofalexandria.com
Or scan the code below: